THE
SECRET
OF THE
HOWLING
CAVE
LEE RODDY

THE SECRET OF THE HOWLING CAVE

LEE RODDY

BETHANY HOUSE PUBLISHERS
MINNEAPOLIS, MINNESOTA 55438

Published by Bethany House Publishers
A Ministry of Bethany Fellowship, Inc.
6820 Auto Club Road, Minneapolis, Minnesota 55438

Printed in the United States of America

Library of Congress Cataloging-in-Publication Data

Roddy, Lee, 1921–
    The secret of the howling cave / Lee Roddy.
       p.   cm. — (An American adventure ; bk. 4)
    Summary: When Hildy finds a stolen watch concealing a crude, hand-drawn map, she is accused of the theft and must try to clear her name.

    [1. Mystery and detective stories. 2. Christian life—Fiction.]
I. Title. II. Series: Roddy, Lee, 1921–   American adventure ; bk. 4.
PZ7.R6Sb   1990
[Fic]—dc20   90–763
                                        CIP
ISBN 1–55661–094–7   AC

To
June Hibdon,
a longtime friend
who has encouraged me
in both my writing and my faith.

AN AMERICAN ADVENTURE SERIES

LEE RODDY is a bestselling author and motivational speaker. Many of his over 48 books, such as *Grizzly Adams*, *Jesus*, *The Lincoln Conspiracy*, the *D. J. Dillon Adventure Series*, and the *Ladd Family Adventures* have been bestsellers, television programs, book club selections or have received special recognition. All of his books support traditional moral, spiritual, and family values.

Contents

Chapter One

Trouble in a Small Town

Hildy Corrigan's troubles began unexpectedly one Monday morning in mid-August. The twelve-year-old girl walked barefoot along the high boardwalk in Lone River. Her pet raccoon rode in the usual place astride the girl's neck, hanging on to the long brown braids that fell to her waist.

"Mischief," Hildy whispered to the coon, "I sure would have liked to get that watch for Molly's birthday. Since I can't afford it, what'll I do now?"

Hildy leaped lightly off the walk on her long, gangly legs, crossed an unpaved alley, and jumped nimbly back onto the board sidewalk.

She plunged tanned hands into the two pockets at waist level of her homemade yellow print dress. The left pocket was empty. From the right she withdrew an old Bull Durham sack and hefted it thoughtfully. It still smelled of the tobacco it had once held. She told Mischief, "Sixty-five cents won't buy much. Mr. Taggett almost laughed when—what's that?"

She whirled, startled, as a man sprang from the alley onto the boardwalk behind her.

"Look out!" he yelled.

Hildy tried to jump out of the way, but it was too late. The man smashed into her. They both staggered and fell.

She glimpsed a scrawny young man in carpenter's white overalls, frayed blue denim shirt, and heavy work shoes. A plaid golf cap hid his eyes.

The raccoon squealed in fright and leaped clear of Hildy's neck. Mischief landed on top of several sacks of rolled barley stacked under the plate glass window of a feedstore.

Hildy sprawled beside the feed sacks, her back crashing into the wall so hard the window rattled ominously. The man ended up on his hands and knees at the girl's feet.

Slightly stunned from the force of her fall, Hildy struggled to her knees, saying, "Are you hurt? I didn't see—"

"Get away from me!" the young man shouted. His fierce command made Hildy draw back against the grain sacks.

The man did not look at her, but glanced furtively around on the boardwalk.

Frightened, Hildy scrambled to her feet and looked for Mischief.

The stranger muttered, "Where'd it go?"

"Where'd what go?" Hildy asked. From behind the feed sacks Mischief growled warningly at the man. Hildy picked up Mischief and held her close to her body.

The man in overalls cried, "If you made me lose that—" His implied threat broke off as an older heavyset man in a baggy suit rounded the alley corner in a waddling run.

Hildy recognized Mr. Taggett, owner of a pawnshop bearing his name. A few minutes before, Hildy had examined his dusty stock of jewelry, spyglasses, china, musical instruments, and similar items. People had "hocked" the items, leaving them as security for money borrowed. Because the people had not returned to pay back the money they had borrowed, the pawnshop owner could sell the objects. That's where Hildy had seen the watch she couldn't afford. In fact, there was nothing in the

Taggett store Hildy could buy with sixty-five cents, so she'd left.

The man in overalls jumped up. "Get outta the way!" He dashed past Hildy, the wooden sidewalk echoing with the pounding of his heavy work shoes.

"Stop him!" Mr. Taggett yelled, waving his arms as he forced his short legs from the alley to the high boardwalk. The pawn-shop owner stood up and waddled toward Hildy. His face was flushed clear up to his bald scalp.

Hildy automatically took a step backward out of the older man's way. Mischief scrambled up on Hildy's shoulder, using the dress pockets as steps.

As the merchant panted past Hildy, he yelled, "Why didn't you stop him?"

Hildy was too surprised to answer. She felt the coon reach her shoulders and take her favorite position on the back of Hildy's neck, furry legs dangling on either side. Hildy didn't look at the pet, but kept her eyes on the two running men.

What's going on? she wondered.

"Stop, thief!" the pawnshop owner shouted at the younger man, who was fast pulling away from the perspiring merchant.

"Thief?" Hildy repeated aloud to herself. She watched the man in overalls dash madly down the boardwalk. He passed a Model T Ford and a spring wagon with a team of horses backed up to the high boardwalk. Except for this sidestreet, the rest of Lone River's streets were paved. The old-fashioned boardwalks had been replaced with lower concrete sidewalks.

The younger man crossed another alley, leaped up to the high boardwalk where it continued, and kept running. The shouting merchant fell farther behind.

A short distance ahead of the fleeing man, the door of Lone River's only coffee shop opened. A tall, well-built policeman in khaki shirt and pants stepped casually out. He rolled a toothpick to the corner of his mouth and started to put on his peaked cap. He tensed and glanced toward the two men running toward him.

"Stop him, Chief!" the older man panted. He waved his arms, shouting, "He stole—" He couldn't finish because he was so short of breath.

The town's only full-time policeman (and therefore the chief) reacted instantly. He dropped his cap and reached for the holstered revolver at his right hip.

The fugitive skidded to a quick stop, pivoted fast, and ran back to the alley. He leaped off the boardwalk and disappeared between the buildings.

The bareheaded policeman followed, running hard and yelling, "Police! Stop!"

The officer, too, was lost to Hildy's sight. Her natural curiosity made her want to stay to find out what was going on, but her father was waiting two blocks away, and he hated to be kept waiting.

"We'd better go meet Daddy," Hildy said to the coon. She turned back the way she'd come. Her blue eyes probed store windows on the unpaved side street of the small California town.

All stores had the NRA Blue Eagle emblem with the words "We do our part." That was another of President Franklin D. Roosevelt's "alphabet" agencies to get people back to work in 1934, the depth of the Great Depression.

"Hey, you!" Mr. Taggett's sharp voice made Hildy stop again. The pawnshop owner was returning from where he'd been staring down the alley. He pointed a stubby finger and asked, "Where're you going?"

"To meet my father. I'm late—"

"You're not going anywhere, you little thief! Stand right there!"

Hildy felt a strange, sickening feeling seize her. "What're you talking about?" she asked in bewilderment.

The merchant thrust his face toward hers, his dark eyes blazing. "Don't play dumb with me, you Okie!"

Hildy's face froze at the insulting name. She had worked hard to lose any trace of the accents common in the Texas Panhandle, where she had picked cotton at age five, or from the Ozark Mountains of Arkansas, where she had lived until about two months ago.

It's because I'm barefoot, she told herself. *That's why he called me an Okie*. Shoes in the Corrigan family were limited to one pair for school and another for church. The rest of the time Hildy went barefoot, like all the kids she knew.

Taggett frowned, studying the girl's face. "I remember you!" he cried triumphantly. "You came into my store a while ago to case the joint! Then you left, told him I was alone with the watch, and he came in and grabbed it!"

"I came in to buy my stepmother—" Hildy started to explain, but the merchant cut her off.

"That's why you didn't stop him! You're in this with him! Wait'll the chief gets back! I'll have you arrested for helping rob me!"

Hildy protested vainly, her emotions racing. She thought, *Wish Ruby were here*, then shook her head. *No, guess I'm glad she's not.*

Ruby Konning was Hildy's feisty thirteen-year-old tomboy cousin and best friend. Ruby had an uncontrolled temper and a quick, sharp tongue. Ruby wouldn't have taken any insults off this man, but Hildy was more calm and rational. She tried to explain, but the merchant only glared at her, warning her not to move.

A few minutes later, the chief returned, breathing hard. He reported that the younger man had escaped. Mr. Taggett repeated his accusation against Hildy. The pawnshop owner concluded, "It was a ladies' antique gold watch with a long, delicate chain to be worn around the neck. It was pawned late Saturday afternoon just before I locked the store for the weekend."

He pointed at Hildy. "She was the first person in the store this morning. She came in to make sure nobody else was around, and just where the watch was. Then she left and sent this man in right away. The only thing he asked to see was that very same watch. When I showed it, he grabbed it and ran. I tell you, Chief, they're in this together. Arrest her!"

Hildy almost moaned in frustration. "I wanted to buy the watch for my stepmother's birthday, but couldn't afford it. And I never saw that other man before! I didn't even see what he dropped."

She explained to the chief exactly what had happened, then led an unsuccessful search around the feed sacks for the missing watch. Finally she stood up and shrugged. "He must have found it before he ran off."

Frightened and fighting angry tears at the false accusation, Hildy persuaded the two men to accompany her to where her father was waiting.

As the three approached, with Mischief riding on Hildy's shoulders, Hildy saw her father pacing impatiently in front of a small auto-repair shop. There was no car dealer in town. Joe Corrigan had driven his borrowed touring car there to see if the garage owner knew of an available secondhand car.

At the sight of Hildy, Joe Corrigan's blue eyes blazed from a deeply tanned square face. He was a rider who worked as a cowboy for the Woods Brothers Ranches east of Lone River.

Hildy saw her father's mouth open to reprimand her for being late. He closed it with a click of teeth upon seeing the officer and merchant flanking Hildy.

"What's going on?" her father demanded, hurrying to meet the trio. Joe Corrigan was a powerfully built man with a two days' stubble of dark beard. He wore his usual sweaty, gray wide-brimmed hat, faded blue work shirt and jeans, with scuffed, pointed-toe boots.

"Oh, Daddy!" Hildy cried, breaking free of the two men and rushing up to him. "Mr. Taggett wants me arrested for helping a man steal a watch! I didn't even get a good look at him, but I know I never saw him before."

The chief took charge. "You Joe Corrigan?"

"Yes, and this is my oldest girl, Hildy." He put his strong arms around her. The raccoon riding astride Hildy's neck made chirring noises in protest. "Now, what's this all about?" Hildy's father demanded, looking at the two men.

"I'm Chief Thorne," the uniformed officer began. "And this is Horace Taggett. He owns the pawnshop on Elm Street."

"Get to the point!" Hildy's father snapped.

"Your little Okie gal helped somebody rob me!" Taggett exclaimed.

Hildy saw her father's eyes narrow and his jaw muscles twitch. "Call her that again and I'll whup ye, mister! My Hildy wouldn't steal anything!" Except when he was angry, Joe Corrigan seldom mispronounced words or reverted to terms common to some rural areas of the country where he had worked.

Taggett stepped back a little from the sudden fury showing in Joe Corrigan's face. "Well, she helped the man that did!"

Hildy's father let go of her and grabbed for Taggett's coat lapels. But the chief had anticipated the move. He stepped between them.

"Now hold on!" the officer said, his voice softening. "Let's go inside where it's shady and talk this over calmly."

The garage had an open pit in the middle of the dirt floor. Tools were scattered along greasy benches. Old California license plates were nailed across knotholes on every wall. A large electric light, heavily flyspecked, hung from the open rafters on a long, twisted cord. Everything smelled of oil and dust.

At a word from Chief Thorne, the owner-mechanic adjusted his oily cap and walked into his small office. He closed the door so the others could talk privately.

"Now," the officer said, "Horace, suppose you tell your side of this to Mr. Corrigan; then his daughter can tell hers."

The merchant retold his experience, his voice rising in anger.

At the unpleasant loudness Mischief stirred uneasily and squirmed out of Hildy's arms. The raccoon jumped to an oily bench, then to the dirt floor and out the door. Hildy started to follow, but stopped when Mischief hopped up on the running board of their borrowed car, through the open window into the backseat. Hildy turned back to Taggett.

The pawnshop owner was saying, "I could tell she wanted that watch, but she only had sixty-five cents. So she left, but in a couple of minutes, a man came in and asked to see the same watch. So he knew I had it.

"When I showed it to him, he grabbed it and ran. I chased him. When I came around the corner by the feedstore, I saw him and this girl talking."

"He ran into me and knocked me down!" Hildy explained,

looking up at her father's stern face. "I tried to tell them that, but they won't listen!"

"Easy, Hildy!" Joe Corrigan glanced down at her and patted her bare arm. Then his blue eyes focused again on the merchant. "Finish your story, mister!"

Taggett nodded. "That's the only watch the man looked at, so he had to know it was there. And since your girl's the only one who could have told him, I want her arrested for helping steal it!"

Joe Corrigan's hands moved so fast Hildy didn't even see them until they gripped the merchant's coat lapels. "I told you—!" Joe began, but the chief interrupted.

"Easy, Joe!" He reached out a restraining arm. "I don't think there's enough evidence to bring that charge against your daughter. Joe, give me your address, then take her home. I'll try to find the young man who got away with the watch."

"Much obliged," Hildy's father said. He released the merchant's lapels and nodded his head respectfully to the chief. "I'll do that."

Taggett angrily waved his arms. "If that watch isn't returned, I'll still file charges against her!"

Joe Corrigan gritted through clenched teeth, "Mister, you bother my daughter, and you'll answer to me! She's no thief!"

"That's enough!" the chief said firmly. "Everyone go on about your business."

On the drive to their place in the country, Hildy absent-mindedly petted Mischief, who had curled up in the girl's lap.

"Oh, Daddy!" Hildy moaned, "I'm just sick about this! Unless they catch that man, Mr. Taggett's going to think I'm a thief—and maybe the chief will too. And if Mr. Farnham hears about this, he won't let me be his hired girl, and I won't be able to save for college!"

"It'll be okay, honey."

Hildy sighed and nodded. She tried to tell herself that when she got home to her family, everything would be all right. She leaned forward anxiously as her father slowed down by a stand of slender Lombardy poplars. He turned into the quarter-mile long dirt driveway. The Corrigans couldn't afford to rent a house, so they lived in a barn.

Hildy expected to see her four younger sisters, their step-mother, and baby brother Joey come out to greet them, but they didn't. Instead, only her cousin Ruby dashed barefoot out of the barn.

Hildy stiffened in sudden concern. "Daddy, look how hard she's running! What else could possibly go wrong today?"

CHAPTER
TWO

MORE TROUBLES

Hildy was out of the borrowed car the moment her father stopped it in the dusty driveway by the barn. She could see tears glistening in her cousin's hazel eyes. Ruby's face was twisted as though in pain.

Hildy dashed across the barnyard and clutched Ruby by both hands. "What's wrong?"

Even barefoot and with blond hair cut in a boyish style, Ruby was an inch taller than Hildy. Ruby wore her usual striped overalls with a boy's faded blue denim shirt. "Oh, Hildy," Ruby moaned, "y'all cain't believe whut he wants me to do!"

"Who?"

"Muh new daddy, that's who!" Ruby spoke with a definite mountaineer accent acquired back in her Ozark Mountain home. "We had a turrible arg'amint!"

"Uncle Nate?" Hildy asked in surprise. Ruby's mother was dead, but for years, Ruby hadn't known if her father, Nate Konning, was alive or dead. Then, just last week, the girls had found him. He hadn't even known he had a daughter. In just a few days, they'd gone from a happy reunion to big trouble.

Hildy glanced at the barn-house to see if Ruby's father was

coming out the door. He wasn't. Neither were Hildy's step-mother and sisters and brother. The barn was silent.

The Corrigans rented the eastern end of the structure called a California hip barn. Rough partitioning had converted the eastern manger area to crude living quarters. Ruby and her father had stayed with the Corrigans since the girls had found him last Friday.

Hildy had expected the newly reunited pair would be very happy. Instead, Ruby was fighting tears.

Hildy studied her cousin quickly and decided they weren't sad tears. Rather, they seemed like angry or frustrated ones. Hildy suggested, "Let's go over in the shade of the barn, and you tell me about it."

Hildy turned back to where her father was getting out of the borrowed car. Hildy saw Mischief jump out of the car's open backseat window. In a waddling, side-to-side run, the coon headed for her favorite hideaway and disappeared in the long tangle of blackberry vines.

The girls reached the shade as Hildy's father hurried up. "What's going on, Ruby?"

"Oh, Uncle Joe!" Ruby's voice began to rise in an anguished wail, "he wants me to—to—" She stifled a sob and didn't finish.

"Nate?" Joe Corrigan asked, frowning. "Get a hold of your-self, Ruby! What's he want you to do?"

She rolled her eyes upward in despair so the whites showed. "He wants me to—to stop dressin' like a boy an' start wearin' dresses!"

Hildy blinked in amazement and exchanged looks with her father. She turned back to Ruby. "You mean—you're upset be-cause of that?"

"Not jist that!" Ruby flared, anger showing in her tone. "He wants me to stop fightin' with boys, an' yankin' their hair out by the roots, and sech things!"

She jerked her right shirt sleeve up and flexed her well-developed biceps. "Ain't nary a boy I know got muscles strong as me! And now he wants me to—to 'start actin' like a lady'— that's the way he put it! An' he wants us to start goin' to church reg'lar! Oh, Hildy, whut'm I a-gonna do?"

Hildy laughed in relief. So did her father.

Ruby snapped angrily, "Y'all a-laughin' at me?"

"Oh, Ruby!" Hildy said, forcing the laughter down and trying to keep a straight face. "You should be grateful to have finally found your father after all these years. Nothing should make either of you unhappy."

"Well, I ain't no lady, and I ain't never a-gonna be, neither! So don't ye start a-takin' his side in this, or ye ain't no kin o' mine!"

Hildy's father also had wiped the smile from his face. "Let's go inside and talk about this." He glanced toward the barn-house door. "Where is everybody?"

"They walked over to Spud's tree house. Some neighbors done dropped off a passel o' dime novels fer us to read. But Molly said they's mostly fer menfolks. So she took the kids an' magazines to Spud's.

"Nate—uh—muh daddy—oh, whut'm I a-gonna call him? Anyhow, he went along with yore stepmother 'cause I'm so blasted mad at him I could spit nails! Molly said it'd be good fer me to have a spell o' quiet time, and I reckon I plumb agree!"

Hildy's father turned back toward the borrowed car. "I'd better go get them. It's getting too hot for baby Joey and the girls to be walking back in the sun. You two had better wait inside where it's cool until I get back."

Hildy had momentarily forgotten her own troubles in Lone River until her father drove off. She wanted to tell Ruby about the watch and Mr. Taggett. The cousins walked along the shade of the weathered barn-house while Ruby continued telling about her troubles.

Hildy listened while absently looking at the barn. The roof line sagged in the middle like an old swaybacked mule. Moss grew on the northern eaves. The high center door to the hay-mow was closed, although the Jackson fork still hung precariously outside on a fraying rope.

At ground level, two large sliding doors were closed at the east and west ends. A glass window had been put in the sliding door at the northeastern end, where the eight Corrigan family members lived.

Hildy slid the barn door open so the girls could slip through. Her stepmother had hung flour-sack curtains over the windows. Hildy was relieved that Ruby didn't have a serious problem like an illness or injury.

She changed the subject from Ruby's complaints by saying, "You'll never guess what happened to me in town."

"Did ye git a purdy present fer yore stepma's birthday?"

Hildy shook her head. She led the way past a fifty-gallon drum of water carried from the nearby tank house.

The original house had burned down, and there was no running water in the barn. Hildy's eyes took in the familiar boxes of pots and pans, a tin-lined woodbox, the wood-burning stove, a cupboard with a box set up to hold a pail of water beside a white, chipped enamel washbasin. There were no beds. The family slept on pallets of old coats and blankets until they could afford regular bedding.

Hildy sat down on the homemade bench and put her elbows on the cracked oilcloth that covered the table. "I almost got arrested for stealing," she began.

"Yore joshin' me!" Ruby exclaimed, sitting down opposite her cousin.

"No, I'm not." Hildy quickly retold all that had happened.

When she had finished, Ruby slammed her open palm down hard on the table. "Wisht I'd a-been thar! I'd a-snatched that Mr. Taggett plumb bald-headed!"

"He's not the cause of it. The robber is. But it's certain Mr. Taggett doesn't like people like us, calling me an Okie and a thief!"

"Then I wisht we could find that feller who run into ye and knocked ye down! I'd whup him so hard he'd ache all over fer a month o' Sundays!"

Hildy smiled at her cousin's strong, defensive attitude. "If I could find the real thief, maybe Mr. Taggett would believe me. But there's no way I could do that. I wouldn't even know where to begin."

"Ye wouldn't, and I wouldn't, but Brother Ben Strong might." He was an eighty-five-year-old former Texas Ranger who attended the same Lone River church as Hildy.

"I never thought about that," Hildy admitted.

"Whut was the watch like?"

"Oh, it was gold, very thin with lots of engraving like fancy initials on the front and back."

"I heerd tell President Roosevelt outlawed ownin' gold when he took office last year."

"Not heirlooms, I guess. That's what Mr. Taggett said this watch was. It was so pretty! It hung on a long, beautiful chain. Molly would've looked good with it hanging around her neck. Oh, and the front and back both opened."

"Whut fer?"

"Well, the front opened so you could see what time it was. The face was white with black Roman numerals for the hours. The back cover opened up to show a picture."

"Whut kinda pi'tcher?"

"A lady. Very old-fashioned looking. Hair parted in the middle. High stiff collar. Picture must've been taken sixty, seventy years ago. Right after the Civil War."

"Hmmm," Ruby mused. "Whar'd the watch come from?"

"Mr. Taggett told me when I first looked at it that a young woman had pawned it Saturday afternoon just before closing."

"He say who she were?"

"No, but it obviously didn't mean much to her, or she wouldn't have hocked it." Hildy sighed. "Boy, I sure wish I could've bought it, but . . ." Hildy left her sentence unfinished and reached into the right front pocket of her dress. She removed the Bull Durham tobacco sack, loosened the pullstring, and poured the contents on the table.

"Sixty-five cents. Been saving that a long time! But Mr. Taggett said the watch was worth fifty dollars."

"Fifty? Why, the highest priced one in the Sears wish book is only $29.95!"

"This was an heirloom," Hildy reminded her cousin, putting the coins back into the sack and pulling the string to shut it. "I didn't get anything for Molly, so I'll have to go back into town soon's I can. Got to get her something else. Only I'm afraid of what'll happen if the police don't catch that crook. Maybe I'll be arrested. And I might lose that job if Mr. Farnham hears about this."

Mr. Farnham owned the town bank, having worked his way up from poverty. He hired underprivileged girls to work in his mansion after school.

"Stop yore frettin', Hildy! They'll ketch that man."

"What if they don't?"

"Then maybe we'uns should ketch him!"

"We?"

"Shore!" Ruby reached over impulsively and touched the back of Hildy's hand. "I'll he'p ye! Then ye he'p git muh new daddy to stop tryin' to change me."

"Well," Hildy said, brightening, "I'll think about that. Now, tell me about your father."

Ruby dropped her voice and glanced around, although there wasn't anyone near. "When muh new daddy gits over this here foolishment 'bout me wearin' dresses and sech like, I'm a-gonna talk him into takin' me back to the Ozarks."

"You mean—to show him off?"

Ruby nodded vigorously. "To show all o' them people that said sech mean, rotten things 'bout me not havin' no daddy. I kin hardly wait to see their faces when they see him. They'll eat crow, ye betcha!"

The mention of Arkansas made Hildy take a slow, thoughtful breath. "I'd sure like to go with you, but there's no way—"

She stopped, feeling the hurt inside. She and Ruby had left the Ozarks barely sixty days before under very difficult circumstances. Hildy tried to shake off the bad memories.

She changed the subject. "I probably should check Mischief over carefully to make sure she didn't get hurt when that man knocked her and me down."

The cousins entered the hot August sun again, walking past the chinaberry tree toward the place where the original ranch house had burned down. They passed the corral, now overgrown with high brown weeds, on past the sheds, the outhouse, and the two-story tank house. The windmill stood silently, waiting for a trace of wind to turn the tin sails.

The cousins approached the stone chimney, the evidence that this was where the original ranch house had stood. Wild blackberry vines now covered the foundation.

"Thar's Mischief!" Ruby said, pointing. "A-settin' on that ol' stump at the far end of the blackberry vines."

"I see her." Mischief came immediately at Hildy's call, so the girl didn't have to risk getting scratched by the head-high, yards-long tangle of vine.

After a careful examination, Hildy said, "Seems to be just fine." She hoisted Mischief to her shoulders, where the little animal gripped the base of the girl's long braids.

Hildy and Ruby were turning back toward the barn-house when Hildy stopped suddenly. "Somebody's whistling!"

Ruby made a face. "That means Spud's a-comin'."

"How could that be? You said Molly and the kids went to his place to—oh, I know! He must've been off someplace but is now heading home."

"I don't know why he cain't jist leave us in peace."

Ruby and Spud had struck sparks from the moment they met, and their relationship hadn't improved.

Hildy waved to Spud, who was followed by his Airedale, Lindy.

"You be nice to Spud!" Hildy warned. She reached up, touched her hair and rearranged the long brown braids so they hung straight down her back.

"Wisht he'd go back to his folks in New York," Ruby growled, following Hildy toward the barn-house and the approaching fourteen-year-old boy.

The girls had met Spud in June while they were still in Arkansas. He said he'd run away from home because his father had been so mean. Spud had arrived in Lone River shortly after Hildy, her family, and Ruby had reached there.

Hildy said to Ruby, "I asked him to write his mother, and he promised he would. Maybe that's what he's coming to tell us about."

"Would ye be sorry if'n he went back to his home?"

Hildy didn't answer, but felt a sudden sadness.

The dog came bounding toward the girls, stub tail wagging, his tongue rolling from the heat. Hildy reached down and gave him a quick pet on his head. "How's Lindy?"

Spud grinned at Hildy as he approached in cowboy boots, blue jeans, and a long-sleeve denim shirt buttoned at the neck and wrists. He normally wore an aviator helmet in imitation of his hero, Charles A. Lindbergh, who had flown the Atlantic alone in a single engine airplane seven years before. Today Spud wore a cowboy hat with tapered crown and rolled brim because of the protection it offered from the San Joaquin Valley's blazing sun.

"Hi!" he called, grinning at Hildy. "Lindy and I were over at the neighbor's helping pick peaches when Brother Ben came along."

Ruby snorted. "Reckon that dawg kin pick peaches good's ye any day."

Hildy jabbed an elbow in her cousin's ribs. The boy seemed not to hear.

"Brother Ben's going to drive up to Thunder Mountain tomorrow to take some food and things to Mrs. Benton, the widow. You know?"

Both girls knew. Mrs. Benton and her children were "squatting" in a Kansas-style dugout on a small ranch owned by Nate Konning.

"So if you want to come along," Spud continued, "Brother Ben said you're welcome." He looked eagerly at Hildy with green eyes that always made her feel a little funny.

Hildy shook her head. "I'd like to go, but I'd better stay close to home awhile." She briefly told Spud about the morning's experience in town.

Before Spud could comment, Ruby looked up. "Car a-comin'! Whoa! It's a po-liceman's!"

Hildy glanced up at the approaching car with the large gold shield painted on the front door. "Oh no!" she cried. "He's coming to arrest me!"

CHAPTER THREE

THE BRUSH ARBOR

The short, heavyset deputy sheriff in light tan uniform introduced himself as Woody Halden. Hildy introduced herself, Ruby, and Spud.

Deputy Halden explained, "Hildy, I'm here because of the Taggett store robbery. Since you live in the county, Chief Thorne asked the sheriff if a deputy would do the follow-up investigation."

Spud asked, "Isn't that because Chief Thorne's jurisdiction is only inside the city limits?"

The deputy nodded. "That's right. The sheriff is responsible for the county. And Hildy, everybody in this county knows about 'the girl with the coon,' so I recognized who you were even though we'd never met. Now, Hildy, I need to ask some questions. Do you want to wait for your parents before my interrogation?"

Hildy shook her head. "I got nothing to hide. But first, let's go over in the barn shade."

Hildy led the way, flanked by Ruby and Spud. They whispered for her not to be afraid.

The officer took out a small note pad and pencil. "Can you

identify the man who knocked you down?"

"No. I told Mr. Taggett and the police chief that I never saw him before."

"Can you describe him?"

"I'm afraid not. It all happened so fast, I didn't even get a good look at him." Hildy added what she could about the man's clothing, then answered the deputy's other questions.

Finally he closed his book, thanked her, and started back toward his patrol car. Hildy, Ruby, and Spud followed him from the barn's shade into the hot summer sun.

Hildy asked anxiously, "Does Mr. Taggett still think I had anything to do with that thief?"

"Legally, he was a robber, not a thief. A thief is one who steals, especially secretly, or without force. A robber takes from someone else by threat or force. But to answer your question—yes."

"But why?" Hildy exclaimed. "Just because he thinks I'm an Okie, as he called me?"

"No, Hildy, he said it's because of the circumstances. The woman who pawned the watch—Alice Quayle—brought it into the shop just before closing time Saturday afternoon. You were the first customer in the store that morning. You looked at the watch, then left.

"Almost at once, this man came in and asked to see that very same watch. He grabbed it and ran. Taggett figures that nobody knew the watch was there except you, and so you told the robber who grabbed it."

Ruby had been unusually silent. She frowned, saying, "Now lookee here, Mister po-liceman, yore fergittin' that maybe this hyar Alice Quayle person done tol' somebody she'd pawned the watch!"

"Chief Thorne is following up on that aspect of the investigation. He'll also talk to her lawyer and the people in his office."

"Lawyer?" Hildy repeated.

"Yes. I understand Quayle had just received the watch Saturday afternoon from her late aunt's estate. The lawyer gave her the watch in his office."

"She certainly didn't waste any time pawning it," Spud exclaimed, "so it must've not had any value to her!"

The deputy shrugged. "Miss Quayle has quite a reputation around Lone River. Her late aunt, Effie Baines, was wealthy. She lived in town near her niece, but there was no love lost between them.

"Effie was a hard-nosed character who came by her family traits from her mother, Clarabelle Rockwell. Both those women held on to every penny, but Effie once told me that Alice was a spendthrift. Everybody knew Effie and Alice didn't get along, so I'm not surprised the old gal didn't leave Alice much."

Hildy asked, "The watch is all that the aunt left?"

Deputy Halden nodded. "Everything else went to another niece back East somewhere. Alice got only the watch, which she promptly pawned. But what none of us yet understands is why that watch alone was taken from Taggett. Well, nice meeting all of you."

Hildy, Ruby, and Spud went back to the shade of the barn and discussed the latest information for a while. Then Spud left, reminding them of Ben Strong's offer of a ride to the foothills.

Spud and Lindy had been gone only a few minutes when Hildy's father drove back with his wife and children. When the car stopped, Hildy and Ruby met them.

Four towheaded girls spilled out of the vehicle ahead of their stepmother, anxiously asking Hildy for details of what their father had already told them.

"Let's go in the house," Hildy replied, putting her arms around ten-year-old Elizabeth and seven-year-old Martha. Sarah, five, and Iola, three, followed.

Inside, the five sisters sat around the homemade table on handmade benches while their stepmother placed the baby, fifteen-month-old Joey, on the bedding.

Their father had left again to look for a car, because soon he had to return the one he'd borrowed. The Lexington Minuteman in which he'd brought his family to California had recently been wrecked.

Molly straightened from the sleeping baby and joined her

stepdaughters at the table. "Now," Molly said, tucking her homemade gray dress under her knees, "let's hear what happened, please, Hildy."

Molly had been a widow whose only child had also died before she married widower Joe Corrigan. Molly was in her middle thirties, a little taller than Hildy but very strong physically. She had brown eyes and light brown hair with a few streaks of gray.

Hildy was tired of telling about the experience in town, but she repeated it, adding the part about the deputy's visit.

Molly reached across the table and patted Hildy's hand. "I really appreciate you trying to buy me a birthday gift, Hildy, but I'm sorry it led to such problems. What I can't understand is why the robber risked taking the watch in the daylight when he could have broken in over the weekend and taken it without anyone seeing him."

Elizabeth, the most practical of the younger sisters, bent forward and shook her bangs away from her blue eyes. "Because he didn't know about it until today, I'll betcha!"

"But if Hildy didn't tell him about the watch, who did?" Martha asked.

Ruby slapped her sturdy hand on the oilcloth so hard she made the kerosene lamp bounce. "That's whut we ort to ask them other people the depity mentioned—the lawyer an' people in his office."

Hildy nodded in agreement. Just then she heard her father's car returning. A little concerned that he was back so soon, everyone went to the sliding barn door. They peered through the small glass window.

"Daddy's bringing Uncle Nate!" Hildy exclaimed. She turned to her cousin. "Daddy must've met him walking along the road."

As everyone hurried through the door and into the barnyard, Ruby grabbed Hildy's arm. "He's been a-lookin' fer a place fer us to live. We cain't stay in yore barn ferever 'cause he's got to find work."

Nate Konning had been a sheepherder when Hildy and Ruby found him last week. He was a tall, slender man with long, untidy blond hair that fell on both sides of his unshaven face. He wore faded hickory-striped overalls, scuffed cowboy boots, and a sweaty tapered western hat.

"Howdy," Nate said with a Texas accent. "Ruby, I found us a place to live fer a while 'til we decide what to do next." He frowned at his daughter's overalls. "I 'spected y'all'd be a-wearin' a dress by now."

Ruby's short temper flared. "I ain't got no dress!"

Her father replied mildly, "Reckon y'all could borry one from yore cousin." He shifted his gaze to Hildy. "Couldn't she?"

Hildy nodded, uneasy at being caught in the unpleasant exchange between her best friend and her newly found uncle.

Joe Corrigan saved the situation from becoming worse. "I'd like to see this place you've found. Everybody pile in, and we'll drive over together."

On the short drive down the graveled road, Ruby was sullen and withdrawn in the backseat with Hildy and her four sisters. When Hildy's father turned down a rutted, dusty lane, the little sisters began chattering.

"It's a big house!" Elizabeth exclaimed. "Under all those trees and everything. Ruby, you're lucky!"

"Uh," Nate said, clearing his throat from where he sat in the front seat beside Molly and the driver, "that's whar the owner, John Shimms, lives. I . . . uh . . . talked to him about rentin' us the chicken house."

"Chicken house?" Ruby exploded. "Ye want me to wear dresses an' live in a chicken house?"

Hildy was embarrassed. She whispered to her cousin, "That's not nice!"

"Don't tell me whut's nice! I ain't never a-gonna live in no chicken house!"

"We live in a barn," Elizabeth said, "and it's not so bad."

Nate took a deep breath and spoke softly. "Joe, would y'all mind turnin' aroun'? Ain't no sense even a-lookin' now."

The drive back was made in cold, stiff silence. Hildy was very upset. She could hardly wait to get her cousin alone to point out a few things about getting along in a family.

The car was within a half mile of the Corrigan barn-house before anyone spoke. Hildy's father lifted one work-hardened hand from the steering wheel to point to the right. "What's that?"

Nate spoke for the first time since they'd turned around. "Some folks are a-buildin' a brush arbor. I talked to the workers a while ago when I was a-walkin' back from our—uh, the Shimms'."

Hildy was anxious to ease the stony tension in the car. She leaned forward in the backseat to survey the brush arbor.

Weathered square posts had been set upright at the four corners, making a wall-less structure about thirty feet long and twenty feet wide. Old two-by-fours had been placed across the top for roof supports. Women in faded shapeless dresses handed up freshly cut apricot and peach branches to men in overalls standing on twelve-foot ladders. The men placed the limbs with green leaves across the two-by-fours. The rude roofing would keep out the fierce August sun. It never rained in the summertime, so there was no need for the leaves to be weather tight.

"When'll they start services?" Hildy asked, joining her sisters in returning friendly waves from the brush arbor workers.

"Tonight," Nate replied. He paused, then twisted in the front seat. "I'm a-goin', and I'd be obliged if'n y'all would jine me."

"I don't much cotton to goin' to reg'lar churches," Ruby snorted, "so I shore ain't a-gonna go hyar!"

Her father sighed. "Reckon I'll go anyhow. Been a powerful long time since I heard the Gospel a-tall."

"Then I'll jist stay an' visit with Hildy," Ruby announced.

"I think Uncle Nate's idea is a good one," Hildy said. "I'd like to go to the service. Wouldn't the rest of you?"

There was a chorus of agreement from everyone except Hildy's father and Ruby.

Joe Corrigan made his excuse. "I've heard about a car that's for trade, so I've got to check that out tonight."

Ruby exclaimed, "I'm a-goin' with ye, Uncle Joe!"

Back at the barn-house, Hildy picked up Mischief from the

den she'd made deep in the shadows of some old packing crates. They'd been covered with gunny sacks to keep it dark. Since raccoons are nocturnal, Mischief preferred to sleep in the day-time, except when she was with Hildy.

Settling the coon on her shoulders and feeling the tiny fore-paws grip the base of her braids, Hildy said, "Ruby, let's go for a walk."

"Okay, but don't try lecturin' me none!"

The cousins walked past the blackberry vines into an open field. "Ruby," Hildy began, "you spent your whole life wonder-ing if you really had a father. Then we found him just last week, and here you are already acting as if you're sorry."

"I tol' ye—don't lecture me none!"

"I'm just trying to talk some sense into you!"

"I don't want nobody tellin' me whut I kin and cain't do! Reckon I been on my own too long to give up muh freedom."

"You want to give up your father and be like you were be-fore?"

Ruby stopped short, her hazel eyes flashing. "No, but I ain't a-gonna let him tell me whut to do, neither!"

"He's your father! The Bible says, 'Obey—' "

"Reckon I'm a-goin' back to the barn-house now," Ruby in-terrupted sullenly.

That evening, everyone except Joe Corrigan and Ruby at-tended the first church service in the brush arbor. Hildy led her family down the freshly laid sawdust aisles. She sat with her family on cottonwood logs that had been stripped of bark and smoothed out to be used as crude benches. A smaller log had been placed as an altar between the front row of benches and the raised platform that served as the pulpit.

A man thin as a stick of rhubarb and dressed in overalls and a clean blue work shirt opened the service with a brief prayer. Then he led the singing with a battered guitar. The favorite old hymns aroused memories of Hildy's childhood, when her mother was alive. Hildy was so caught up in the power of the gospel songs that she momentarily forgot her troubles with Mr. Taggett and Ruby's problem with her father.

After the singing there was a brief testimony period before the same thin man laid down his guitar, opened a limp black Bible, and began to preach about the need for salvation. Hildy had made her own commitment to the Lord earlier this summer. Her thoughts drifted to her troubles over the missing watch.

If the police don't find it, she mused, *everybody's going to think I was involved. I've got to clear my name, somehow. And I will!*

The decision made, her mind returned to the service. The lay preacher wiped his perspiring brow with a huge rumpled handkerchief. He waved his arms and cried, "If the Lord has been speaking to you tonight, dear brothers and sisters, now's the time to come forward, kneel at this altar, and get right with Him!"

Only one person moved. Nate Konning stood slowly, as if in doubt. He shook the long hair from his face and stepped out into the sawdust spread on the aisle. With obvious growing determination, he hurried to the altar and dropped to his knees.

Hildy turned in surprise to her stepmother. She smiled approvingly, the baby asleep in her arms. The two younger sisters were sleeping on the bench beside her.

Hildy leaned across in front of Elizabeth and Martha. They were quietly drawing on a pad Molly had provided. Hildy whispered to her stepmother, "Wonder how Ruby's going to take this?"

About half an hour later, Nate Konning raised his head. Through the shaggy hair that spilled down both sides of his face like hound-dog ears, Hildy saw bright tears glistening on his cheeks. But his face was radiant, and Hildy knew the reason.

Still, Nate was strangely quiet on the walk home. He carried the two youngest sisters. Molly carried Joey. Hildy helped the two older girls, who were half-asleep.

As they turned into the Corrigan driveway, Nate spoke. "I not only done recommitted my life to the Lord tonight, I also settled an old call to preach."

"What?" Hildy exclaimed.

Before Nate could reply, Ruby burst from the barn with a lantern in her hand.

"Hildy!" she screeched, running down the lane with the lantern bouncing wildly, "me'n Uncle Joe jist got back, and somebody done tore the place to pieces! We been robbed!"

CHAPTER
FOUR

MYSTERY OF THE WATCH

Ruby was right. By the lantern's weak light and a coal-oil lamp that Joe Corrigan had lit and set on the table, Hildy could see what a mess the burglar had made.

The covered barrel of water kept just inside the door had been tipped over. Boxes of pots and pans and a cupboard had all been emptied onto the floor.

Molly gasped, "Oh, Joe! What a mess! Why would anyone do that to us? We haven't got a thing worth stealing!"

Her husband closed the door of the empty icebox, which the burglar had left open. The family couldn't afford ice. "Beats me, but it sure makes me mad clean through!"

Ruby pointed to the pallet of old clothes and blankets where her Aunt Molly and Uncle Joe slept. "Whoever done this plumb tore up yore beddin'!"

"And ours!" Hildy added, glancing at the tangled mess of tossed quilts and old coats along the north wall near the sliding door. She had slept head-to-toe with her sisters on a pallet that was now soaked with water.

Nate Konning turned from where he had been standing in a small doorway that opened into the other part of the barn. "Looks like whoever done this scattered Ruby's and muh beddin' all over, too. He even turned over the straw and empty boxes out here, too. But why?"

"My money!" Hildy exclaimed, seeing the dress she'd worn that morning crumpled in a corner. She splashed through the water and scooped up her dress. Anxiously, she plunged her fingers into the pocket. "It's still here!"

She withdrew the Bull Durham sack, opened the pullstring and emptied the coins into her left palm. "Every penny's here! Whoever did this threw my dress from the nail to the floor, so he must've heard the coins—so why didn't he take them?"

Nobody had a logical answer. They continued the search, straightening up as they could.

A little while later, Molly sat down at the table and stared thoughtfully into the pale yellow coal-oil lamp. "Nothing seems to be missing, so why'd somebody do this?"

"I think I now know why," Hildy said thoughtfully. As everyone turned to look at her, she explained. "Whoever did this was after the watch I wanted for Molly."

Her stepmother protested, "But you said the robber got it after he bumped into you!"

"That's the only thing I could think of, but apparently he didn't. So he must believe I found it. He must have waited until none of us was home. Then he looked for it here."

Hildy's father agreed. "It's the only thing that makes sense. But if the crook thinks you have the watch, that means . . ." He let his voice trail off.

Ruby finished the thought. "It means Hildy's in danger from that thar varmint whut done this!"

In the excitement, Hildy hadn't thought of her raccoon. "Mischief!" Hildy suddenly exclaimed. "Anybody seen her?"

Nobody had. Hildy searched in the barn and outside, calling for Mischief, but she didn't come. Hildy felt a little sick in her stomach. "If he hurt Mischief—!"

Hildy's father broke in. "Mischief probably just hid when the robber broke in. She'll turn up." He got up from the table and stretched. "Well, I've got to work tomorrow, so let's try to straighten this bedding out enough for all of us to get some sleep."

Hildy's half of the bedding was too soaked to use. She found some dry musty-smelling comforters in an old metal steamer trunk. She pulled out enough for herself and Ruby, but the floor by the door was too wet to sleep on.

"Why don't you older girls sleep outside behind those gunnysacks Elizabeth and Martha tacked up for their play-house?" Molly suggested.

Joe Corrigan and Nate Konning agreed it was probably safe. Whoever had burglarized the place almost surely wouldn't be back. Hildy and Ruby helped get the younger girls bedded down. Then Ruby picked up the lantern, and Hildy took the bedding.

Ruby's father said, "Good night, everybody." He looked at his daughter and added tenderly, " 'Night, Ruby."

Ruby seemed not to hear. Hildy sensed the tension between her uncle and cousin. Hildy started out the door, saying good night to everyone, including Ruby's father. He nodded and headed into the main part of the barn where he had been sleeping. The moment Ruby slid the barn door shut, Joe blew out the lamp inside.

The night was very dark, and the lantern didn't give much light. At the eastern end of the barn, Hildy pulled aside a corner of the sacks to shove the bedding through and onto the ground.

The younger sisters had ripped old sacks along the seams and spread them out wide. Two walls had been made by tacking one end of the sacks to the barn wall. Stakes had been driven into the ground to hold the other ends. There the cousins spread out their bedding.

It was too hot for a cover, so the girls lay down on top of the bedding. Ruby blew out the lantern, and the darkness settled over them. There was no roof, so the girls could see the sky. It held millions of stars but only a thin crust of moon.

Hildy whispered, "Sure is pretty."

"An' peaceable," Ruby agreed. "Not a-tall like things down here on earth."

Hildy wanted to tell Ruby about her father going to the altar at the brush arbor, but decided that was something Uncle Nate would want to tell Ruby himself.

Hildy was also tempted to repeat what Nate had said about answering an old call to preach. Again, Hildy was sure that was something she shouldn't tell. Not now, especially, with Ruby being so angry toward her father. She'd let him tell Ruby in his own way and time.

"Why the big sigh?" Ruby whispered in the darkness.

"Huh? Oh, I didn't realize I'd even done that."

Hildy dismissed thoughts of the trouble that was sure to come when Ruby and her father discussed what he had done tonight. Hildy couldn't help those problems, but she might help herself with her own.

Ruby mused aloud, "If'n the crook don't have the watch, and ye don't, then whar is it?"

"I don't have any idea."

"Ye reckon Mr. Taggett'll really have ye arrested?"

"I hope not! Oh, Ruby, it's such a terrible feeling to know you didn't do something that somebody else says you did— especially when they want to arrest you!"

"Yore name'll shore be drug through the mud, all right. Small town like this, ever'body soon hears about ever'body else. Even Mr. Farnham'll—"

"Mr. Farnham!" The words exploded from Hildy's mouth. She jerked herself upright. "I forgot about him!"

"Reckon he won't likely let ye be his hired girl an' work in his fancy big mansion if'n he hears yore under suspicion like this."

"Oh, Ruby!" Hildy moaned, lying down again. "If that happens, I'll be ruined. I was counting on getting that job! It's the first step in my plan to go to college and someday get our 'forever' home!"

"Quiet down out there so's the rest of us can sleep!" Hildy's father called from inside the barn-house.

The girls fell silent, but Hildy's mind whirled in anguish. She folded her hands on her chest and looked up at the stars. She said a silent prayer. Then she slept.

During the night Hildy awoke with a start. She sat upright, her heart pounding. Out of the corner of her eye, she saw that Ruby was also sitting up. The pale moon had set, leaving only cold, distant stars for light. Both girls strained tensely to hear again whatever sound had awakened them.

The crook! Hildy's mind screamed. *He's come back!*

Hildy expected to hear a man's footsteps. Instead, she heard a chirring noise and nearly collapsed with relief.

"It's Mischief!" she whispered, reaching down to lift the far corner of the gunnysack. Her fingers closed on the raccoon's soft fur. Instantly, she felt something cold and strange. She dropped both coon and object, jerking her hands back in surprise.

"What's matter, Hildy?"

"Light the lantern! Quick!"

Ruby fumbled sleepily to obey while Hildy stared at her pet's vague outline. Hildy tried vainly to decide what strange object her fingers had touched.

When the kitchen match flared, Hildy saw a reflection in Mischief's right forepaw. By the time Ruby had touched the lantern wick for more light, Hildy saw what it was. "The watch!" She reached out and grabbed it. Mischief protested with little annoyed sounds. The coon loved bright, shiny objects. "It's the same watch I saw in the store!"

Ruby held the lantern close. "It's mighty purdy! But how'd Mischief get it?"

Hildy frowned, thinking back. "The man must have stolen the watch, and when he bumped into me, he dropped it and then Mischief snatched it. When I picked Mischief up again, she could have dropped the watch into one of my dress pockets. But I was so used to the coins in the pocket, I didn't feel the weight of the watch."

"Reckon yore right. Lemme see it."

In a moment Ruby let the long gold chain slide through her fingers while she opened the engraved front. "Ain't that somethin'?" she exclaimed, staring at the bold black Roman numerals on a white porcelain face. Then she unsnapped the back.

"Lookee here! It's a woman's pi'tcher! Must be that Clarabelle . . . whatever-her-name-was the depity mentioned. Mean-lookin' ol' lady, ain't she?"

As Hildy took the watch, the faded brown photograph fell out. She recovered it from her lap and started to replace the picture, then stopped. "Hold the lantern closer, please, Ruby."

Both girls leaned forward to study the back of the photograph. A crude, hand-drawn diagram in faded brown ink had been sketched there many years before.

Ruby said, "Looks sorta like a map."

"I think you're right, but a map of what? Those lines don't look like roads. That part with the X looks like it's in a room or something. Only it's a round-like room, not a regular square one."

"Yore shore raht! Wonder whut the X means? See? It's thar at the bottom of that—!" She interrupted herself to exclaim, "Hey! That kindee looks somethin' like a drawin' o' George Washington! Ye know, sorta like the one we had in school back home in the Ozarks."

"There's some writing," Hildy said, moving the map closer to the lantern light. "Very old, almost faded away. Looks like two capital initials: *H.C.*, I think."

"No, they's another letter after the *C*, maybe a little *n*. *H.Cn.* But I cain't be shore!" Ruby turned the picture over to again look at the faded photograph. "I never seen no pi'tcher that old!"

"Must be one of the first made. I remember reading about pictures being taken of soldiers in the Civil War. But I don't think they took portraits like this until after the war. It ended in 1865."

Ruby mused, "Ye reckon this here drawin' on the back o' the pi'tcher is whut the robber was after, an' not the watch itself?"

Hildy pushed Mischief aside and started to crawl out of the sack shelter. "Could be! I've got to show Daddy."

"Ye better not do that! He'll be powerful mad if'n ye wake him up now. He ain't goin' to git none too much sleep nohow 'cause o' the mess that feller made, breakin' in an' all."

Hildy felt her heart skip a beat. "You think that man will come back tonight?"

"Ain't hardly likely! Way he tore this place up, he must shore figger it's not hid here."

"You're right. Well, I'll tuck it here under our bedding so it'll be safe. We'll tell the deputy in the morning. Then my name'll be cleared."

Ruby blew out the lantern. "Reckon yore right."

The girls lay down. Hildy petted Mischief absently, feeling a lot better about things. She finally drifted off to sleep.

In the morning, she awakened to the distant sound of roosters crowing. She opened her eyes, felt Mischief's warm furry body by her neck, then remembered the watch. Hildy felt under the bedding, blinked, then felt again.

Ruby opened her eyes and asked sleepily, "What'sa matter?"

"Don't tease me, Ruby! Where's the watch?"

Instantly Ruby was wide awake. "I didn't touch it! Honest!" She joined in the search, but it was useless.

Soon Hildy groaned, "The watch is gone! But where'd it go? Mischief, did you take it again? Or did the crook come back and—?"

When Hildy and Ruby burst into the barn-house with the startling news of what had happened, Molly was feeding Joey. Hildy's father had left for work before dawn.

Nate Konning came out of the main part of the barn, unshaven, his long hair hanging down on both sides of his face. He and Molly joined the girls in their search.

It was hopeless. They abandoned their efforts and stood frustrated outside the barn-house in the cool morning air.

Hildy moaned, "I'm right back where I started—only worse! Mr. Taggett'll never believe we found the watch and then it disappeared again! What'll I do now?"

When the other girls were awake, they helped conduct a thorough search, but there was no trace of the watch.

Hildy made a decision. "I'll walk into town and find out who the lawyer was that the deputy mentioned. Then I'll go tell that lawyer exactly what happened."

"Good idee!" Ruby exclaimed. "Git him to tell Mr. Taggett whut happened. If'n ye go to Mr. Taggett direct, he'll plumb have ye behind bars quicker'n ye kin say 'scat'! I'll go with ye."

Hildy was a little reluctant to have her sharp-tongued cousin along on such a delicate mission. Still, Hildy was secretly glad for company. After some discussion with the adults, Hildy put on shoes and her only Sunday dress. Ruby did the same, except for the dress.

As the girls started for the door, Hildy heard a car coming. She looked out the small door window. A big yellow Packard was pulling up in the barnyard.

"It's Brother Ben!" Hildy cried, sliding the heavy door open and running outside.

Ben Strong was a tall, stately man with white hair and large white handlebar mustache tinged with yellow. He stepped out from under the wheel of his 1929 Packard Victoria. It had black fenders, brown canvas top, and whitewall balloon tires mounted on bright red spokes. The matching spare tire in brown covering rested in the well to the base of the right front wheel. It was an elegant car, and totally in keeping with the six-foot four-inch former Texas Ranger's present success.

"'Mornin'," Ben said in his soft, easy drawl. He held a big white cowboy hat in large, strong fingers. "Spud delivered my message, I see. You girls ready?"

Quickly Hildy explained everything that had happened from yesterday morning in Lone River to this morning in the gunny-sack playhouse.

The old ranger turned back to his car. "Get in, girls. I'll drive you in to the lawyer. I know him—Seth Rawlins. Got a young law clerk named Merle Lamar. We'll square this away so Hildy can get on with her life."

Seth Rawlins' law office was upstairs over Lone River's only bank. As Hildy, Ruby, and Brother Ben walked along the empty hallway, their feet echoed strangely. The old ranger explained that the other offices were empty because of the Depression. Hildy smelled fresh paint as she followed the stately white-haired man through a door with a frosted glass window.

A young man with pock marks on his sallow cheeks looked from behind a desk as the trio entered the outer office. The old ranger introduced him as Merle Lamar, then turned back to hang up his hat.

"So you're Hildy Corrigan?" the clerk asked, his nose crinkling as though he smelled something bad.

"Yes," she replied. "We'd like to see Mr. Raw—"

The clerk interrupted. "I know who you are!"

"You do?" Hildy didn't remember meeting Merle Lamar.

"Yes! You're the girl who stole the watch!"

CHAPTER FIVE

BAD NEWS KEEPS COMING

Hildy was so surprised she jerked as though slapped in the face. She tried to speak, but couldn't. She turned abruptly to leave and bumped into Ruby, who was standing just behind her.

Ruby stepped around Hildy and leaned over the law clerk's desk. "Why, ye no-good-fer-nothin' polecat! Whar'd ye git off a-talkin' that way?"

Hildy was so upset she almost bumped into Brother Ben, who turned from hanging up his hat. "Whoa, there!" he called softly. "Where you going?"

"How could he say such a terrible thing?" Hildy cried, fighting tears. She rushed out the door with the frosted glass window into the empty hallway. Her Sunday shoes clicked loudly, sending echoes back from the stairwell.

She was so hurt at the totally unexpected and cruel remark that she leaned against the nearest door. When it yielded to her weight, she almost fell. She caught her balance and stumbled inside. The office was empty except for a ladder, a man at the

45

top with a brush in his hand, and dropcloths on the floor.

"Oh!" Hildy said, trying recover from the verbal hurt the law clerk had inflicted on her. "I'm sorry!" The smell of fresh paint was overpowering.

"Nothin' to be sorry about!" the painter assured her heartily. He was in his middle twenties, a little stocky, with a white billed cap, paint-splattered overalls, and a shirt buttoned at neck and wrists. He smiled down at her, the paintbrush suspended in midair. Then his smile vanished. "Anything I can do for you?"

Hildy shook her head, the long braids flying. Through the adjoining office wall she could faintly hear the law clerk's voice.

"Mr. Strong, I'm terribly sorry! I shouldn't have said that to her." Hildy heard a swivel chair's rusty springs squeak. "Of course I'll go find her and apologize!"

Ben's voice commanded, "Hold on there! You tell me something first, then go find her and apologize."

Hildy thought, *I don't want to talk to that terrible man!* She spun and shoved the door shut, then took a quick step to the left so her silhouette wouldn't show through the frosted glass in the door. She leaned heavily against the wall and laid her finger across her lips. "Shh!" she whispered to the startled painter on the ladder.

A moment later she heard the law clerk's leather heels hurrying down the hallway. He called her name, adding apologies. When his footsteps sounded near the stairwell, Hildy looked up at the painter.

"I'm sorry," she said in a small, hurt voice. "I'll go just as soon's he's far enough away."

He nodded and said with a hint of concern, "There's a back stairway. He can't see you go out that way."

"Thanks!" Hildy opened the door slightly, listened, then slipped out. She ran on tiptoes the opposite way she'd come up. She reached the top of the backstairs and started down them just as the lawyer's office door opened. She heard the voices of Brother Ben and Ruby, but Hildy didn't slow down. She hurried on and out the back door.

Some time later, Hildy saw the old ranger and Ruby heading

toward the yellow Packard. She waited until she was sure the law clerk wasn't following; then she ran down the sidewalk and slipped into the backseat.

The stately driver flipped the underside of his handlebar mustache with the back of his right finger. He steered the car with the other hand. "Hildy, I can't understand how he could have said that. He's new and obviously no credit to his employer. I told him I'm going to tell Seth Rawlins what happened. That young man's a disgrace to the profession he plans to enter!"

"Ye shoulda let me whang him alongside his haid, Brother Ben!" Ruby said from the right front passenger's seat. "I'da l'arned him manners!" She turned to look at Hildy. "Ye want I should sit back thar with ye?"

Hildy shook her head. "I'll be all right," she said, sniffing. "It just was so unexpected, so unfair."

"Brother Ben got that thar clerk feller to tell us whar the niece lives—the one who pawned the watch," Ruby said. "We'uns air a-goin' thar now to talk to her, if'n ye don't mind."

Hildy didn't mind. In fact, she was glad for the opportunity to learn more about the cause of the problems that threatened her happiness.

The Packard soon stopped in front of a modest frame house in need of paint.

Hildy's eyes were red, but otherwise she had gained her composure when she and Ruby followed the old ranger up to the door. He knocked, and a young man opened it. Hildy caught a faint, unpleasant odor she couldn't identify.

Brother Ben asked, "Is Miss Alice Quayle in?"

For a moment the man at the door regarded the visitors without speaking. He was very thin, wearing a fine three-piece blue serge suit. He wore the most fashionable shoes—black and white oxfords.

Hildy wondered what he did for a living, because it wasn't Sunday, usually the only time men in Lone River wore suits. In spite of his elegant appearance, Hildy wrinkled her nose at the faint smell about him.

Finally the young man asked, "Who wants to know?"

Hildy was jarred by the blunt question. She was still smarting from the law clerk's remark. She fixed the thin man with a firm gaze. "I do!" she snapped. "Hildy Corrigan, the girl accused of stealing the watch Miss Quayle pawned. I've got to talk to her—now!"

The man drew back sharply, staring at Hildy, his mouth working a moment before answering. "Okay! Okay! Don't get huffy!" He turned and called, "Alice! I think you'd better come here."

The snappily dressed man opened the door slightly, and a young woman appeared beside him. She wore an all rayon dress that fell just above her ankles. A crocheted hat, very smart with a soft brim dipping over her right eye, let freshly marcelled blond curls peek out from under the left brim. "I'm Alice Quayle," she said with a puzzled look at the three strangers on her porch.

Hildy introduced herself, Ben Strong, and Ruby, then added, "I'd like to talk to you about the watch you pawned last Saturday."

"Don't talk to her, Alice!" the young man said softly.

Hildy had suffered enough humiliation for one day. She said crisply, "I think you'd better, Miss Quayle. My name's being ruined because of false accusations that I helped steal that watch. I'm going to clear my name, and I'd appreciate it if you helped!"

Alice hesitated, then nodded, "Come in." She pushed the door open. "Don't mind him. He's just trying to protect me. His name's Bob Medwin. We were on our way out, heading for The City."

Hildy nodded, recognizing that in California "The City" meant San Francisco.

Hildy followed her hostess past a twelve-tube radio console just inside the living room door. Through the open kitchen door, Hildy glimpsed an electric refrigerator with the round mechanical unit on top.

The flowered wallpaper in the living room was peeling, but the ceiling appeared to have been newly painted. Hildy noticed an upright telephone on the coffee table by the sofa when she sat down. Brother Ben sat on her right, his white cowboy hat over his knee. Ruby sat on the left.

When Alice Quayle and Bob Medwin had seated themselves on occasional chairs facing her, Hildy quickly explained her reason for coming. She covered everything from bumping into the man with the watch to finding it in the night and having it disappear by this morning.

Medwin's hands twitched. "You sure you didn't get a good look at the thief?"

"Positive. It all happened so fast." Hildy turned to the young woman. "Now, I'd appreciate if you told me everything you can about the watch."

"Nothing much to tell," the hostess said, pulling one of two tasseled cords on a brass-plated floor lamp. The scalloped shade had transparent rose-colored cloth with hand-painted pink flowers and green leaves.

"Tell us anyway, please," Hildy urged.

"Well, it belonged originally to my great-aunt, Clarabelle Rockwell. She was quite a character, I understand. Moved to Lone River before the Civil War and was among those who tried to get California to secede from the Union and form an independent nation friendly to the South."

Hildy didn't know much about California's role in that war, except she remembered California had been admitted as a free, non-slave-holding state. But this wasn't the time to ask history questions. She said, "Yes, please go on."

Alice Quayle nodded. "Great-aunt Clarabelle left the watch to her niece, Effie Baines. She was my aunt, who died recently. Clarabelle and Effie were both well-to-do. Even in this Depression, Aunt Effie managed to hang on to most of her money. She lived across town, but we didn't see each other much. She didn't like me, and let me know it. I was surprised she even left me the watch when she died."

Hildy asked, "Is it true that you received the watch last Saturday from the lawyer and went right to the pawnshop with it?"

"Sure! Why not?" Alice Quayle's voice took on a sharp, defensive tone. "It was mine, but I had no use for it, so I hocked it. I'm using the money for this trip."

"Did you open the watch, Miss Quayle?" the old ranger asked in his slow, easy manner.

"I opened the front and saw it had big black numerals on a white face. I thought it was ugly."

Hildy almost held her breath to ask, "You didn't open the back?"

"The back?" Alice Quayle blinked in obvious surprise. "I didn't even know it opened."

The young man stirred. "Look, Alice, if we're going to get to The City on time—"

"We're leaving. Thanks for your help," Hildy interrupted, standing quickly.

At the doorway, Alice asked, "What was in the back of that watch?"

"I assume it was a picture of your great-aunt."

Hildy started to explain about the sketch on the back, but Alice interrupted. "It's just as well I didn't see her face! When I was little, she was mean to me. Always making cutting remarks. Well, I'm sorry the watch's lost again, but I can't say I care much, personally."

"One more question, please!" Brother Ben said. "How'd your great-aunt first come into possession of the watch?"

Alice laughed. "That's a family scandal! When we were kids, we heard that Great-aunt Clarabelle was the girlfriend of some outlaw. He robbed stagecoaches up in the Mother Lode. He supposedly gave her the watch. 'Course, it's probably not true, but it's a good story."

———

As the old ranger headed the Packard back through town toward the highway leading to the Corrigan's place, Hildy's mind whirled. "It's so hard to believe how complicated my life's become the last couple of days. And all because of that—oh,

Brother Ben! There's Mr. Farnham! Please stop! I need to talk to him."

The Packard eased to the curb. Hildy jumped out to greet the owner of the local bank as he walked along the sycamore-lined sidewalk.

Matthew Farnham was a small, dapper man who always dressed nattily. He wore an expensive Panama straw hat, light gray summer suit, and white shoes. He was one of the few well-to-do men in Lone River.

"Mr. Farnham," Hildy began, managing a smile as she approached him. "Remember me? Hildy Corrigan? You interviewed me as a hired girl at your home."

The banker eyed her thoughtfully over oblong-shaped, silver-framed bifocals. "I remember you very well, Hildy! I was most impressed with you in our interview. I always admire young people who plan to make something of themselves in spite of this terrible Depression. Maybe that's because I also came from humble beginnings. However, I won't make a decision on that position until closer to when school starts. I'll let you know."

That brief conversation perked up Hildy's spirits. As the Packard left Lone River, Hildy said, "Brother Ben, remember once when you told me everybody needed more than a goal? They also needed a purpose, a plan, and perseverance?"

"I remember, Hildy. Is that helping you get that 'forever' home you've been wanting for your family?"

"It will, starting with getting that part-time job with Mr. Farnham after school. Everything depends on starting to save money for college!" Hildy paused, then added, "But right now I was thinking of how to clear my name in this watch-theft situation. I'd welcome any suggestions you have."

"Why don't you ride up to Widow Benton's with me when I take her and the children some food and clothing the church donated? We could talk on the drive."

"Wonderful! I'll check with Molly when we get home."

Hildy didn't get an opportunity to do that. When the Packard stopped at the barn-house, Martha came running out, her tow-head reflecting the sun.

"Hey, Ruby!" the seven-year-old cried, "what'd you think about being a preacher's kid?"

Ruby stepped off the running board into the dusty yard with a frown. "What air ye a-talkin' about?"

Hildy scooped up her little sister quickly, gently sliding fingers across the girl's mouth. But she twisted her head aside and blurted, "Uncle Nate is gonna be a preacher man!"

Ruby exploded, "He cain't do that! He ain't even a Christian!"

"Is so!" Martha cried, twisting her head to avoid Hildy's fingers again. "Last night at the brush arbor he give his life to the Lord. He says God called him to preach!"

Ruby's shock was so genuine that she turned pleading eyes to Hildy. "That ain't so, air it?" She paused, seeing the truth in her cousin's eyes. Ruby's voice rose to a screech. "Ye knowd, an' ye didn't tell me, Hildy?"

"I thought it was better if Uncle Nate told you," Hildy said lamely.

"Ye done me wrong, Hildy! Ye shoulda tol' me! An' my daddy done me wrong, too! He cain't jist go a-makin' decisions like that without a-talkin' to me! He's a cowboy, not a preacher!"

Ruby's angry, piercing voice brought the other Corrigan sisters out the barn door. They were trailed by Molly, carrying baby Joey. Nate Konning came last. He had shaved and cut his long hair. It was parted it in the middle and greased down in shiny neatness.

"Ruby," he began, rapidly approaching her, "I wanted to talk to ye last night, but the burglary—"

"Air it true?" she interrupted, hazel eyes bright with anger. "Be ye a-gonna take up preachin'?"

"Ruby, honey, let's go someplace whar we kin talk."

"I don't never want to talk to ye agin!" Ruby spat the words at her father, then whirled on Hildy. "Ye knowd, and ye didn't tell me! That makes ye a party to this, an' I won't never fergive ye!" She turned and ran back to the Packard.

Hildy called anxiously, "Ruby, where you going?"

"I don't know, an' I don't keer! Brother Ben, I'd be obliged if'n ye took me outta their sights!"

"Wait!" Hildy called. "Please wait!"

Ruby leaped onto the running board, slid into the right front seat and slammed the door.

The old ranger said quietly, "I'll talk to her."

Hildy nodded numbly and watched the yellow vehicle head down the long, dusty driveway. A terrible ache filled Hildy from head to toes. She stared after Ruby in shocked disbelief.

Then she heard a sad, lonely voice beside her. "I barely found muh dotter! Now I done lost her!"

"She'll be back," Hildy assured him.

But she wasn't sure. That uncertainty, along with Ruby's angry parting words, added more pain to Hildy's already overloaded life. She was sure it was going to get worse.

CHAPTER SIX

A STARTLING DISCOVERY

After Ruby and Brother Ben had gone, a terrible sadness engulfed Hildy. Molly had the four younger sisters play outside while the others went inside the barn-house. It had been pretty well cleaned up after last night's burglar had ransacked it.

Nate Konning sat on the nearest bench, facing away from the table. He bent and placed his head in his hands. He moaned through the fingers, "Why wouldn't she jist give me a chanct to 'splain things to her?"

Hildy took off her Sunday shoes and stockings before walking over to him. She lightly placed her hand on the distraught man's shoulder. "Uncle Nate, I guess I know Ruby better than anybody else does, so maybe I can help you understand her."

Nate raised his head, and Hildy saw tears glistening there. She began, "You remember what we told you after we found you? I mean about people tormenting Ruby all her life because her mother had died and everyone said she had no father?"

"I 'member, Hildy, but I didn't even know I had me a dotter!

I didn't know 'til ye found me last week at Thunder Mountain."

"Ruby knows that. But you weren't what she was expecting her father to be . . ." Hildy didn't finish.

"You mean, 'cause I was a sheepherder when I used to be a cowboy?" Nate knew that in cattle country, it was considered a terrible thing to slide from being a buckaroo to herding sheep.

"She thought you were a rider, like my daddy."

"I was, but I was also like Jonah, runnin' from God. Ye see, I was saved at a camp meetin' in Texas. That's whar I met Beulah, Ruby's mother. I felt God called me to be a preacher, but I didn't want to be one. Beulah begged me to foller my leadin'. I backslid. Started drinkin'. Things got so bad Beulah done went back to the Ozarks. I heard tell she died. I didn't know 'bout the baby. Anyways, I drank so hard an' drifted so much that finally thar weren't nobody that'd hire me as a rider. So I herded sheep."

Hildy impulsively kissed her uncle on his cheek. It felt strange to kiss his clean-shaven face. "I'm glad to know that, Uncle Nate," she said. "Now let me tell you about Ruby. She spent her life fighting—with words, with fists and teeth and fingernails. She dressed like a boy and acted like one too. She lived with her grandmother in the Ozarks—Beulah's mother. Grandma Skaggs was as mean and ornery as her sister, who's my grandmother Dunnigan. Granny Dunnigan did a terrible thing to me, so Ruby and I ran away together. We ended up here in Lone River."

Molly stepped over and lightly touched Hildy's cheek. Hildy sensed that was because her stepmother appreciated the fact that Hildy hadn't told everything about the reasons the family was now in California.

Hildy looked at her uncle and continued. "Ruby's used to going anywhere, anytime. She's used to fighting her own battles. But she's not used to having anybody tell her what she can or can't do. You want her to wear a dress and act like a lady. I'm sure she's glad somebody really cares, but she's still very independent."

"I see," Nate said thoughtfully. "So when she heard I planned on becomin' a preacher—"

"It was too much for her," Hildy finished. "One more thing: She wants to return to the Ozarks and show you off, to make all those people eat crow for having said such cruel things about her all those years. But she wasn't expecting you to be—you know."

"Don't she believe in God?"

"Of course, Uncle Nate. She also believes in the Bible. I've heard her defend it. But she's just not a committed believer yet, and she resists becoming one."

"Thankee kindly, Hildy." He stood and squared his shoulders. "I got a powerful lot o' things to ponder. 'Sides all the problems we jist mentioned, I know a preacher man's got to bring honor to God. So I got to learn to talk better, and eddycate muhself and sech like. But, since God done called me, I reckon He kin he'p me knock off muh rough edges."

Molly said, "And He'll bring Ruby around, too!"

"Just give her time," Hildy added. "Brother Ben'll probably get her to calm down; then everything'll be all right."

Hildy was wrong. About midday the next day, Brother Ben's big yellow Packard whirled into the driveway at an unusually fast speed. Hildy ran outside, her hands covered with flour. She had been helping Molly make chicken and dumplings.

The old ranger got out of the car, swept off his white hat, and looked at Hildy, Molly, and Nate. The younger Corrigan children came running up barefooted.

"I'm right sorry to say this, but Ruby wouldn't listen to me. I took her to a lady, Miz Alden. You met her at church, Hildy. She said Ruby could stay there last night. But this mornin', Miz Alden sent me word that Ruby had run off."

There were startled exclamations from Molly and Nate, but Hildy had a comforting thought and said, "I know where she went; I'm sure of it. The Widow Benton's. Ruby ran off once before and ended up there."

After some hurried preparations, Hildy and Nate headed out the barn-house door toward the Packard. Hildy was happy to see Spud come whistling up the lane with his dog Lindy. When Hildy explained what had happened, Spud asked if he could ride along, although usually he and Ruby didn't get along. But Hildy welcomed a chance to talk with Spud.

The Packard left the flat San Joaquin Valley behind and climbed into the foothills of the towering Sierra Nevada Mountains. Brother Ben sounded his horn going around curves as the law required motorists to do.

Hildy said, "I remember making this same trip before, when Ruby was along. That was before we found you, Uncle Nate. But it was at the dugout we saw a picture of Ruby's mother and knew you'd lived there, although you weren't around, only Mrs. Benton and her children."

Hildy turned to look at Spud. "On that drive, I asked if you'd written your parents, and you said yes but there'd been no answer."

"I wrote again this week," the boy shrugged. "Just so you'd quit asking."

Hildy smiled at him. "I'm glad! And on that trip, I told you I'd written my Granny Dunnigan, but she's never answered, either. Ruby said she plans on going back to the Ozarks to show off her daddy."

Spud looked at Nate Konning in the front seat. "When're you planning on going back?"

"It'd be real hard in this Depression, but if'n muh dotter wants, I reckon I'm obliged to take her. 'Sides, I'd admire to meet muh mother-in-law."

"That's Ruby's Grandma Skaggs," Hildy explained to Spud. "My grandmother Dunnigan and Ruby's grandmother are sisters, although they haven't spoken in years."

"Just like my family and me," Spud said.

Hildy exclaimed, "You know what I'd like? To see everyone reconciled. Spud, you and your family. My grandmother and I. Ruby and her grandmother, and both grandmothers, the sisters—"

"And me an' muh dotter," Nate interrupted.

"Yes," Hildy said soberly, "and Ruby and I."

Spud grinned, his green eyes bright with teasing. "Hildy, I'm surprised you didn't include Ruby and me in your reconciliation plans."

Hildy thought about saying, *I've been praying about that*, but decided to say nothing. Like Ruby, Spud wasn't comfortable with spiritual things, although he'd never told Hildy why.

Brother Ben lifted his hand from the steering wheel. "Thunder Mountain coming up. Be at Mrs. Benton's—uh, your ranch, Nate, in a few minutes."

Soon the old ranger turned the Packard off the county gravel road. He guided the car slowly along a rutted and treeless lane that led straight toward Thunder Mountain, a flat-topped mesa of volcanic origin. It rose massively before them like an ancient castle. At its base, barely visible except for the chimney, a Kansas-style sod house or dugout showed above ground.

"No sign of anybody," Hildy said. "Must all be inside. Sure hope Ruby's there." Hildy turned to her uncle. "When we drove in here the very first time, Ruby saw Mrs. Benton and her children, and you know what she said?"

"Who? Mrs. Benton or Ruby?"

"Ruby! She said, 'My daddy's done remarried! That must be his wife and chillern. Oh, I never expected no secha thing!'"

As Nate chuckled in amusement, the dugout door exploded outward like a storm cellar back home. Four barefooted children poured out, yelling happily and waving. Hildy recognized the oldest, Jacob. He was ten and still wore overalls, although the knees had been patched with material that didn't match. Behind him came three younger girls in frayed dresses.

"Hi, Jacob!" Hildy called, leaning out the window and waving as the Packard slowed. "Hi, Rachel!" She was seven. Rhonda was four. The two-year-old girl carrying a Coca-Cola bottle by the nipple was Becky.

"Ruby's here!" Jacob cried, jumping up on the running board as the car stopped in a cloud of dust. "Only she said to tell y'all to go away. She don't want to see none of y'all a-tall."

"I'll try talking to her anyway," Hildy said, glancing at Nate Konning.

He shook his head. "No, Hildy. That's muh place. I shoulda talked to her before. Then maybe none of this woulda happened."

He got out of the car as Mrs. Benton emerged from the dugout.

She was still as skinny as Hildy remembered, and she was still barefooted and wearing a shapeless old dress. But her hair was neatly combed and put up in a bun. Her rimless eyeglasses were pushed well up on her nose. When she spoke, there was life and hope in her words. "Howdy, ever'body. Light an' sit a spell."

Everybody else emerged from the car and greeted one another. The children wanted to know where Hildy's coon was. She explained that Mischief had been left at home because Hildy had started for Thunder Mountain so suddenly. The kids wanted to play with Lindy. Spud agreed, cautioning Jacob that the dog didn't like boys very well, although he loved girls. Jacob said he'd stay and visit with the company. His sisters ran off to romp with Lindy.

"Mrs. Benton," Hildy said, "Uncle Nate wants to talk to Ruby alone. Is she in the house?"

"No, she done went to the cave."

"The cave?" Hildy repeated.

Jacob explained, "Yeah! They's a swell ol' cave down the road apiece. Called Howling Cave. Ol' Mister Shanley owns it. Ma won't let me go in. But if ye do, Hildy, maybe Ma'd let me go in with ye."

"Hold on, Jacob!" Hildy said with a smile. "I hate small places. You couldn't get me in a little cave."

"It's not little." Jacob waved his hands expansively. "It's bigger'n the whole world, practically! An' Mr. Shanley says it's been there thousands of years."

"Hildy, are you claustrophobic?" Spud asked.

"I haven't looked that one up in the dictionary you loaned me, but if it means am I afraid of closed places, the answer's yes. No caves for me!"

Mrs. Benton explained, "Odell Shanley tol' Jacob some of the rooms air so big ye could put a railroad locomotive in 'em. But it's also got some tiny little tunnels an' things. I won't let none o' my kids go there. Might git lost forever."

A sudden thought hit Hildy. "Ruby—has she ever been there?"

Jacob nodded vigorously. "Ruby ain't skeered, I betcha!"

"Mrs. Benton," Hildy said, "would you let Jacob show me the way there? I promise I won't let him go in. I just want to find Ruby."

The widow nodded. "Reckon I unnerstand. She done tol' me whut happened. Mr. Konning, I'm plumb sorry the Lord's callin' done caused ye this trouble."

Hildy grabbed Jacob's hand. "Come on! You can tell me about the cave on the way over."

"Me, too," Nate Konning said, swinging into step with the girl and smaller boy.

"I'll come too," Spud said.

Brother Ben flipped the back of his mustache and smiled. "Miz Benton, would you mind me keeping you company?"

"I'd be tickled plumb pink, Brother Ben. Come in outta the sun and I'll pour ye a glassa cool water right out o' the crick."

By the time Hildy and the others reached the small shack where Odell Shanley lived by the cave's mouth, Jacob had told the whole story. A gold miner had accidentally discovered the cave in 1850. It was originally called Howling Cavern because wind whistling through the opening made a mournful sound, especially at night.

"Mr. Shanley says outlaws—he called 'em road agents— used to rob stagecoaches an' hide the gold in the cave," Jacob said. "Cain't go in durin' the winter, though," he warned as they neared the cabin. "Mr. Shanley says it's got a couple underground rivers. In the summertime, they's low, so's ye kin step acrost 'em. In wintertime, they fill up so much they even flood the rooms. That's a pity, too, 'cause Mr. Shanley says the water raises so high it changes the President's face little by little."

"The President's face?" Hildy asked.

"President Washington. Mr. Shanley says they's one big room in the cave that looks jist like Washington from all the drippin' an' things over thousands of years."

The sagging door on the shanty swung out on leather hinges.

A bowlegged little man with a wild white beard and crumpled hat stepped out on the sagging wooden porch. Hildy tried to peer inside the open door to see if Ruby was there, but the room was in shadows.

"Hello," the cave owner called, smiling. "I'm Odell Shanley. Call me Odell. Want to see Howling Cavern?"

Hildy was surprised that the man didn't speak with an accent of some kind. Instead, he sounded rather educated.

Hildy started to say they were looking for Ruby, but stopped abruptly. She frowned. "Howling Cavern, you said? Not Howling Cave?"

Odell nodded, his untidy beard flying. "That's what the old-timers called it. Why'd you ask, young lady?"

"Uh, nothing!" Hildy exclaimed, her mind jumping back. She saw again the rough sketch with the initials on the back of the woman's picture in the missing watch.

President Washington! she thought. *And what was it Jacob just said about the President's room? Of course! That's it! And 'H.Cn' on the map must stand for Howling Cavern. Wait'll Ruby hears that. Maybe she'll get over being mad at me.*

The sudden realization that Hildy had a major clue to the mystery of the stolen watch almost made her forget how she and Ruby had last parted.

Then Ruby's bitter, hurt words flashed back into Hildy's mind. "Hildy, I don't never want to talk to ye agin! An' I won't never fergive ye!"

CHAPTER
SEVEN

OUTLAW GOLD?

Hildy tried to stop thinking about Ruby's threat and turned to her uncle while Odell Shanley was babbling away about the cave to Spud and Jacob. Shanley didn't seem to mind the other two not paying attention.

"Uncle Nate," Hildy whispered, standing close to him, "what if Ruby won't listen to me?"

"I tol' ye afore, Hildy. It's muh place to talk to her. She's muh dotter!"

"But she's mad at you, too!"

"She's had time to git over her mad spell." Nate turned from Hildy and raised his voice. "Odell?"

"Ready to see the cave?"

"Not raht now, thankee kindly. Uh—we're lookin' fer Ruby Konning. She's muh dotter."

"You must be Nate Konning. Ruby told me about you."

Nate nodded and introduced Hildy and Spud. Odell bobbed his head in acknowledgment, then chuckled. "Ruby's an opinionated young woman! She told me a little about having an argument with you two."

Odell turned and pointed toward the side of the mountain,

which was not as brown and barren as most of the other foothills. Instead, there were a few spreading valley oaks, a couple of small rounded blue oaks, and a half dozen blue-gray digger pines.

"You'll find Ruby sitting inside the cave mouth by the iron barred gate," Odell said. "That's so people can't sneak in without paying the dime admission."

Hildy and her uncle walked rapidly toward the cave. Spud and Jacob sat down on the rickety steps of the shack to continue talking with Odell.

Hildy saw that the top and sides of the north-facing cave entrance were slightly mossy. The opening was high enough to walk into without having to bend over. Upon entering the cave's mouth, Hildy felt a rush of cold air from deep inside the cavern.

As she and Nate stood at the entrance, letting their eyes grow accustomed to the darkness, Hildy didn't see Ruby. Then Ruby moved, and Hildy saw her cousin's silhouette against the iron gate.

"Hi," Hildy said uncertainly. "I'm sorry about yesterday."

"Same here," Nate added. "I'm plumb sorry I didn't tell ye raht off 'bout ever'thing."

"Go 'way!" Ruby's words were low but firm.

Hildy's eyes could now make out her cousin, who sat on the end of an upturned fifty-pound lug box. Ruby did not look up, but stared into the cave's dark interior.

Nate cleared his throat nervously. "Ruby, jist listen! Ye don't have to say nothin' 'til I finish. But listen! Okay?"

"I said, 'Go 'way'!"

Hildy sensed her uncle drawing back from the sharp edge of his daughter's voice. Hildy tried another approach. "Ruby, I know part of the secret to this cave."

Hildy thought she saw Ruby stir slightly. She plunged on, "Did you know this place used to be called Howling Cavern, not Cave? And that outlaws used to hide their stolen gold and things in here?"

Hildy paused, but there was no answer. She added, "And that there's a room in this cave that looks like a picture of George Washington?"

Ruby remained silent.

Hildy tried again, feeling a little desperate. "Don't you see, Ruby? The sketch in back of the watch was a map! The lines that didn't quite look like roads probably are other ways in and out of this cave. And the X on the drawing of George Washington—"

"Is whar it's hid!" Ruby finished the sentence. She leaped up from the box and rushed toward her cousin and father. "Oh, Hildy! Ye reckon that's whut that's all about? Remember whut Alice Quayle said? 'That's a family scandal! When we was kids, we done heard tell that Great-aunt Clarabelle was the girlfriend of some ol' outlaw, who give her the watch.' "

Hildy smiled with relief. She reached out to touch her cousin's hands. "I remember. If we can just—"

"Gold!" Ruby broke in, swinging around and running to grip the iron bars on the cave's door. "That's why somebody's after the watch." She spun back to face Hildy, her face shining. "Outlaw gold! It's bound to be in this here cave. If we'uns kin find it fust, we won't never have to be po' folks never agin nohow."

"Ruby, yore fergittin' that President Roosevelt last year outlawed ownin' gold," Nate said. " 'Sides, the price o' gold is now only aroun' thirty dollars an ounce, an'—"

"It don't matter none!" Ruby interrupted. "Whatever they is of it, it'll be enough so we kin go back to the Ozarks in style. Drivin' a real autymobile. Why, we'll make them mean old folks waller in the dirt like a razorback hog! We'll . . ." Her voice faded. "Oh," she ended limply, remembering her anger at her father.

When Nate gently reached out and took Ruby's arm, she angrily shook it off and stepped back.

"Ruby, we got to talk!" Nate urged.

"Don't never want to talk to ye!" the girl snapped, folding her arms across the bib of her overalls in a defiant and angry gesture.

Hildy lowered her voice. "Speaking of talking, Ruby. We have to be careful who hears what we just said about the watch and everything."

Ruby hesitated, then dropped her arms. "Okay, we talk, but

only on account o' we got to figger how to git that thar outlaw gold an' be rich!"

"We don't know that it's gold, or an outlaw—"

"Oh, hesh up, Hildy! Let's go talk." She glanced up at her father and added, "Reckon y'all kin jine in, only I ain't never gonna be no preacher's kid."

Hildy closed her eyes briefly and said a quick prayer of thanks. Then she cautioned Ruby not to say anything in front of little Jacob. "Wait'll we're in the car heading back to the valley."

"Ain't a-gonna go back down thar!" Ruby snapped. "Gonna live up here with the widder woman! I like her, and she likes me!"

Hildy and her uncle talked earnestly to Ruby, finally persuading her to return to the valley with them.

"But I'm only a-gonna do it so's we kin talk about findin' that thar gold," Ruby warned. She glanced at her father, a challenge in her eyes. "I ain't gonna change my mind about bein' no preacher's kid."

Back at the dugout, Hildy saw Mrs. Benton put her skinny arm around Ruby and announce, "Ruby is a reg'lar angel in disguise!"

The Benton children agreed heartily, then reluctantly returned Lindy to Spud as everyone got back into the big Packard. The kids jumped up on the running board to reach inside and feel the rich upholstery.

Mrs. Benton smiled at the stately driver. "Brother Ben, much obliged fer bringin' the groceries up. An' please thank the ladies at yore church fer the clothes they sent. With school 'bout to start, I reckon maybe this year my kids'll all git to go fer a change."

She paused, then added, "Speaking of church, they's a nice one down the road a piece. Well, the buildin's nice, but old. Folks been a-fuedin' an' a-fightin' so long they done drove all the preachers off an' most o' the people who used to attend. Down to 'bout ten reg'lar people now, even though they's lots o' people livin' back in these foothills. Me'n my kids been thar sometimes, but we hate all the bickerin' and ever'thing. Too bad they ain't got the right spirit an' a preacher whut won't tuck his tail an' run. If y'all air a-mind to, ye kin see the church on yore way back to the highway. Take a little dogleg gravel road to the right where the high-tension wires cross this road."

Hildy stole a glance at her uncle. Had there been a spark of interest in Uncle Nate's eyes about what the widow had just said? Even if there had been, Hildy decided, Uncle Nate was in no position to say anything that might make Ruby still more angry.

Ben headed his car back toward the main highway. As they approached the tall steel structures that supported high-voltage wires, Hildy felt the Packard slowing.

Ruby stirred in the backseat as the car turned to the right. "Whar're we a-goin', Brother Ben?"

"I want to see this church Mrs. Benton mentioned."

Hildy heard her uncle give a little sigh. She sensed that he also wanted to see that divided church. He leaned forward as the yellow vehicle moved slowly along, raising as little dust as possible. The Packard topped a small hill, revealing what the Forty-Niners called a "flat."

In the shadow of Thunder Mountain, two unpaved country roads met at an intersection. The Packard was on the road running east and west. The other road, running north and south, was empty of all life. Both roads had wide shoulders for parking.

"There's the church!" Hildy pointed ahead. "See it?"

It was a simple white frame building with a small porch in front, a lean-to in back, and two outhouses at the far end, opposite the unkempt cemetery. The large empty churchyard had lots of parking area for cars and hitching for horses.

"Sort of sad-looking," Hildy murmured. "But sort of peaceful and beautiful, too."

Nobody else spoke as Brother Ben eased the car into the silent churchyard before the stark white building. Hildy wondered how long it had been since the bell in the open tower under the small cross had rung.

Hildy felt Ruby stirring uneasily as the Packard almost

stopped, then turned and headed back out onto the road and headed west.

There was something hauntingly lonely about the place that made Hildy turn and look back. She saw her uncle looking back too. Nobody spoke until the Packard reached the high-voltage lines and turned right, heading home.

"Hildy, let's talk more 'bout whut ye tol' me at the cave," Ruby said.

Hildy was reluctant to do that just now. She took one last look back toward the silent, lonely church. Hildy seemed to sense something she couldn't explain or understand. It was like a silent promise, but a promise of what? Hildy shook her head, trying to dismiss the strange feeling. "Everybody here knows part of the story already," she said to Ruby.

"What story?" Spud asked.

"Don't go a-gittin' on yore high horse, Spud!" Ruby snapped, "We're gonna git to that in jist a minute."

"A sophism!" Spud replied, using one of the big words he liked to use—especially to agitate Ruby.

"Whut's that s'posed to mean?" Ruby snapped.

"Easy!" Hildy cautioned. "You two try to get along!"

Ruby nodded but glared at Spud. "Hildy thinks she's fig-gered out why that fancy watch is a-causin' so much trouble. Tell 'em, Hildy."

As Hildy explained, she was pleased to see that Ruby joined in with excited comments. It seemed as if Ruby was forgetting to be angry, but yet Hildy knew the issue wasn't forgotten. This was just a temporary truce.

When Hildy had finished, Spud asked, "What makes you two think that whatever was hidden in that Washington place is still there? Maybe somebody else found it ages ago. Besides, if it's still there, what makes you think you could recover it? The cave belongs to Odell Shanley, so whatever's found there is his, not the finder's."

"Thar ye go agin—a-tryin' to wreck a body's hopes!" Ruby almost spat the words at Spud.

Hildy reached over and gripped her cousin's arm, but Ruby

shook the hand off. "He makes me plumb mad! Always a-tryin' to throw cold water on ever'thing."

"I'm just being practical," Spud growled.

Brother Ben's soft drawl eased the tension. "Seems to me that everyone should be free to say what's on his mind. Look at all the facts. Then it's easier to know what to do next."

That suggestion seemed acceptable to the others, so the discussion continued until everyone had exhausted ideas and thoughts.

One by one, voices fell silent. After a long pause, Hildy summarized. "For me, it all comes down to one thing: Until that watch is found and returned, I'm still under suspicion of being involved in a robbery. I've got to clear my name. In the meantime, we can think about the right thing to do concerning the map. At least we've seen it and know what it means—well, sort of anyway. But whoever's after the watch obviously doesn't know what the map shows, or they wouldn't need the watch."

"So," Ruby mused, "we still got to find that thar watch afore the crook—whoever he is—finds it."

"Unless the responsible party actually recovered the watch while you girls slept," Spud said.

Ruby turned angrily to Spud. "Thar ye go agin!"

"Well, you don't know that the raccoon recovered the watch!" Spud snapped. "So the only alternative is that some reprehensible thief purloined it!"

"Ye make me so blasted mad with yore fancy words!" Ruby roared. "I'm a-mind to—"

"Easy, Ruby!" Hildy grabbed her cousin's hand as she doubled it into a fist. "Let's change the subject."

The others agreed, but Ruby was still angry. She glowered at Spud. "Why don't ye go home to New York?"

Nate Konning cleared his throat nervously. "Ruby, honey, I reckon yore only a-speakin' out so hard against Spud 'cause yore mad at me. I'd be obliged if'n ye'd lay off'n him and light into me, if'n that'd he'p."

Ruby turned her anger toward her newfound father. "If'n I do, will ye give up askin' me to wear dresses?"

"Dresses air only a symbol, I want ye to unnerstand," Nate replied. "Tell ye whut, Ruby. Ye wear one dress a whole day. If'n yore sorry, I'll say nothin' more 'bout it."

Hildy held her breath anxiously as Ruby considered that.

Finally, Ruby nodded. "I'll do it fer one day if'n ye'll listen to me 'bout why ye should give up this wild talk 'bout a call to preach! Then ye kin put that outta yore mind, an' I kin go back to wearin' overalls and sech like. Fair enough?"

Hildy didn't mean to voice her sudden concern, but the words leaped out before her uncle could reply. "Uncle Nate, you can't give up this call to preach! Not again, after all the terrible things you've been through since you tried to run away from God before." Hildy turned back to her cousin. "And you shouldn't ask him to do that!"

"He shouldn't ask me to wear dresses an' act like a lady, neither!"

"I have an idea that should settle this apart from Ruby and Nate's personal feelings." Spud said. "Remember Gideon and the fleece? Why not put a fleece before the Lord on this?"

"I know that story!" Ruby cried. "Yeah! Let's do it—only I git to choose the fleece!"

Hildy felt a wave of fear sweep over her.

CHAPTER
EIGHT
—

A TELEGRAM IS
ALWAYS BAD NEWS

S pud, I think that's a raht good idee—long's I git to choose the fleece!" Ruby repeated.

Her father looked concerned. "I'm not a-tall shore we'uns air s'posed to lay fleeces before the Lord these days. That's testin' Him 'stead o' trustin'."

"Air ye afraid?" Ruby promptly challenged her father. "Afraid if'n we put out a fleece that ye'd lose, an' find ye wasn't s'posed to be no preacher man, after all?"

Before Nate Konning could answer, Brother Ben looked in the rearview mirror at everyone. He voiced his thoughts. "As I recall Gideon's story, an angel was sent to him, telling him to do certain things. But Gideon first wanted a sign."

"That's right," Hildy agreed. "That was the first of three signs. In the first one, the angel touched his staff to an offering Gideon made, and fire came out of the rock and burned up the offering. Later, when Gideon was getting ready to fight against Israel's enemies, he asked God for a second sign to show that he was going to save Israel through him."

"Absolutely correct!" Spud added. "That was when Gideon first proposed that he put a wool fleece on the floor. If dew was only on the fleece side the next morning and the bottom was dry, that was his confirmation. The next morning, the fleece was exactly as he had asked. Still, Gideon wasn't satisfied. He asked God to 'let me prove'—I remember the exact words—and have the opposite results on the fleece the next day."

Hildy looked at Spud with admiration. "I didn't know you knew so much about the Bible."

"Just because I'm not in the habit of regular attendance at worship services doesn't mean I haven't read the Bible," he replied.

"Same here!" Ruby explained. "That's why I know that thar story, too. Next time, Gideon wanted the fleece dry on top an' dew on the ground. An' it were so the next day."

Ruby turned to her father. "Did ye hear whut Spud jist said? Gideon wanted to prove if'n God really wanted him to go do somethin'. So whut's wrong with doin' the same thing now?"

"Ruby, honey, I'm not askin' the Lord to prove my call to me," Nate answered.

"Well, I shore am!" Ruby said emphatically. "Now, air ye a-gonna accept or not?"

"How about t'other way aroun', Ruby? Will ye accept the fact the Lord's called me to preach if'n this fleece—whatever it is—confirms it?"

As Ruby hesitated, Hildy said, "That's only fair."

Ruby remained silent a moment longer; then her face lit up. "Yeah, reckon yore right! That's fair since I git to choose the fleece." She looked around at everyone, her eyes shining with an idea. "'Member that church whut we jist saw? If'n they'll let ye preach a service thar, and if'n the place is packed tight with people, then I'll believe yore call an' won't never fight ye on it agin."

"Oh, Ruby!" Hildy protested. "How could you ask such a thing? You heard what Mrs. Benton said. The church's divided so badly that only a few people come. They don't even have a pastor anymore."

Ruby folded her arms across her bib overalls and said firmly, "That's the fleece! I ain't gonna have no other."

Hildy groaned and tried to reason with her cousin, but it was useless. Hildy sensed that her uncle was praying silently in the front seat.

"Hildy, I said no!" Ruby snapped. "Stop pesterin' me!"

Hildy took a slow, deep breath as her uncle turned and looked back. His voice was low, almost weary. "Ruby, honey, if ye'll agree to abide by this one fleece an' not ask fer another, like Gideon done, well—I'll accept yore word. We'un'll use yore fleece."

A look of triumph spread over Ruby's face. Hildy turned away, feeling sick inside. She sadly shook her head and lapsed into silence that lasted all the way home.

Four more hot summer days slipped by. August was more than half over. Ruby's father got a part-time job feeding livestock on a nearby ranch. His arrangements included room and board for himself and Ruby, so Hildy didn't see her cousin for a while.

Hildy heard that Uncle Nate had asked Brother Ben to write some letters to the church at Thunder Mountain. School would open the third week in September, so Hildy helped Molly finish sewing dresses for Elizabeth, Martha, and herself. But all the time Hildy's fingers worked on the fabric, her mind worked on many problems.

Once Hildy stopped and picked up Mischief from where the racoon was about to taste the red pin cushion. "You won't like a mouthful of pins," Hildy told the coon. "Here, play with this scrap of cloth."

Hildy picked up a stub of pencil and writing pad. She wrote "Prayers" at the top of the page, then listed them.

1. Need more money for Molly's birthday gift.
2. Find missing watch; learn its secret.
3. Daddy needs a car. Return borrowed one.
4. Spud to hear from his family and make up with his father.
5. Granny Dunnigan didn't answer my letter. Should I try to go see her and patch things up if Ruby and Uncle Nate go back to the Ozarks?

6. Help me to clear my name so Mr. Farnham will let me work part time as his hired girl so I can start saving for college.
7. Help me get the forever home I promised the kids.
8. Help Ruby and her father work things out.

Hildy deliberately didn't write down anything about the fleece her cousin and uncle had agreed upon, feeling sure that it would have a sad ending. She didn't want to pray for something she didn't believe would happen.

Three days later Hildy heard a motor vehicle coming down the long driveway. The engine didn't have a familiar sound, and the Corrigans didn't get too many visitors.

"Company comin'!" Elizabeth exclaimed, looking up from where she was playing with paper dolls.

Molly dropped the scissors where she was cutting out a dress pattern. "Martha, see who it is. Hildy, Elizabeth, help me straighten up!"

Hildy hastily plunged her needle into the red pin cushion, shoved the partially made blue dress into a drawer and started shoving things out of sight. Elizabeth helped her mother.

Seven-year-old Martha announced from a crack in the sliding barn door, "It's Uncle Nate and some lady I don't know."

Hildy hurriedly cleared the table of cloth scraps so she could go see who the lady was, but Martha let out a startled exclamation. "That's no lady! That's Ruby, and she's wearing a dress!"

Hildy ran to the barn door and slid it open enough to see. "It *is* Ruby! In a dress!" Hildy slid the barn door open and squeezed through, followed by the other children.

Uncle Nate Konning was just getting out from behind the wheel of an old topless Model T Ford. Ruby was already standing on the ground. She was barefoot as usual, but otherwise looked very different.

"Ruby!" Hildy exclaimed, running up to her cousin. "It's pretty! You're pretty!"

Ruby spun rapidly. "Ye really like it?" The pale green skirt flared above her ankles, the white polka dots flashing in the sun. The short-sleeved top fit snugly. A small, nearly brimless straw hat with a white band was perched at a perky angle on her short blond hair.

"It's perfect!" Hildy replied, clapping her hands in approval.

"Lady whar we'uns air a-stayin' he'ped me make it."

Sarah, Hildy's five-year-old sister, stared at Ruby, then turned to Molly in surprise. "Ruby's growing boozooms!"

"Shh!" Molly said in embarrassment, reaching down to place a hand lightly over the little girl's mouth.

Hildy saw Ruby flush. It was something Hildy had never seen her cousin do. That surprised Hildy almost as much as the dress.

Ruby folded her arms across her upper body as she often did when wearing bib overalls. "I told Miz Gilbert it fit a mite too soon, but she jist laughed. She said it was 'cause I was growin' up and wasn't used to dresses. But ye really truly like it, Hildy?"

Hildy nodded enthusiastically. "I love it!" She turned to Ruby's father. "And look at you, a new suit."

"Not new, hand-me-down," he corrected her politely. "Mr. Gilbert give it to me. Was his brother's afore he died."

Hildy nodded in understanding. In this Depression very few people had new clothes, especially suits. If a garment was usable, it was put back in service, regardless of its history.

"Come in out of the sun and tell us what's been going on since we last saw you two," Molly said.

"Well, to start with," Nate said as everyone headed toward the barn-house, "my boss done loaned me this ol' flivver to drive, and me'n Ruby air a-gittin' to know each other some."

"Actually, we's gittin' along like stray dawgs and cats," Ruby added. "Howsomever, we did both say we air plumb sorry fer bitin' and snappin' at each other like we done. Him an' me air a-tryin' to be sociable-like. Oh, an' guess what? He's got a invite to preach at that thar church."

Hildy stopped dead still, feeling the color drain from her cheeks. "You're kidding?"

"Purely the gospel truth," Ruby said, raising her right hand. "We'uns air a-gonna see how that thar fleece turns—oh!"

Hildy turned to see what Ruby had spotted. "It's Spud and Lindy!" she cried.

Hildy guessed the boy and dog had cut across a pasture behind the barn. They hadn't been seen until Spud bent to crawl through the barbed wire fence. Lindy scooted under the lowest wire. Their coming hadn't been announced by Spud's usual cheerful whistling.

"Hi," Spud called, straightening up. "I—oh, sorry! I didn't know you had visitors."

Hildy started to identify the guests, but Ruby's strong hand gripped her arm quickly and squeezed out a warning. "Shh," Ruby whispered. "Don't say nothin'."

The Airedale bounded forward as always to thrust his head under Hildy's hand.

Spud approached more slowly, frowning slightly. "Well, Hildy," he said, still some distance away, "aren't you going to introduce us?"

Hildy didn't know what to say, for her cousin's hand was still firmly gripping her wrist. Spud came on, a slow smile spreading across his face as he looked at the girl in the polka-dot dress.

Suddenly he stopped so fast one foot was still up in the air, like a bird dog on point. He lowered his head, peering out from under the wide-brimmed cowboy hat he wore as protection from the fierce sun.

"Ruby?" he asked in disbelief, still staring. "Is that really you?" When she nodded, he sputtered, "Incredible transformation!"

Ruby stiffened defensively. "Whut's that mean?" she demanded, letting go of Hildy's wrist and doubling her fists.

"It means I can't believe the way you've changed!" Spud explained.

"Ye sayin' somethin' nice, Spud?" Ruby asked a little uncertainly.

"If I can extricate myself from the abyss in which I've previously placed myself in our relationship, Ruby, I'd say I was never so pleasantly surprised in my life."

Ruby started to smile tentatively. "Ye mean—ye like whut ye see?"

Spud nodded. "I never saw you in a dress before," he said, still staring. "I mean, you always were like a boy. I mean, with overalls and—uh—" He dropped his eyes in embarrassment.

Hildy saw Ruby tilt her chin triumphantly and smile in a way Hildy had never seen before. She felt her insides start to churn. A strange, unpleasant feeling crept over her. She spoke quickly, "It's too hot out here. Come on inside." Hildy tried to make it sound like a normal invitation, but there was an edge to her voice that she had not meant to show.

Ruby turned slowly so the skirt flared slightly above her ankles. She entered the barn-house first, followed by the four younger Corrigan girls, then Molly, and Nate.

As Hildy started too, Spud said, "Uh, Hildy, could you stay out here a moment, please?"

She nodded, wondering what he wanted. If it was to apologize for the silly way he'd acted with Ruby—

As the others disappeared into the barn-house, Hildy fought uneasy emotions as she waited for him to speak.

"Here." He thrust a yellow envelope into her hand.

She glanced down and caught her breath in surprise. "A telegram?" She raised her eyes in sudden concern because telegrams always meant bad news.

"Just arrived. From my mother. She wants me to come. Says my father's very ill."

Hildy gulped hard and glanced at the envelope again. "I'm so sorry, Spud!" she said in a whisper. Then she realized something and snapped her head up sharply. "Are you going?"

"Yes, Hildy. I came to say goodbye."

CHAPTER
NINE
—

A HAND IN THE DARK

Hildy had to swallow twice before she could ask the question that leaped to her mind. "Are you coming back?"

Spud shrugged. "I don't know. My old man and I never got along. He was always knocking me around and cussing me out and saying I'd never amount to anything. I don't want to go, but my mother's telegram—"

"You must go!" Hildy interrupted. She impulsively reached out and touched his hand. "For your mother's sake. And yours. And even your father's. He may want to make things right between you before—I mean—"

"It's all right, Hildy. Personally, I think he's too obstinate to die, but I don't want to have a guilty conscience, so I'm going to do the right thing."

"I'm glad! I mean, that you're going to do the right thing. But I hope you'll come back, even though your family's back there, and you should be with them."

Spud managed a wan smile. "You want me to come back in spite of the uncharacteristic way I behaved with Ruby a minute ago?"

Hildy turned away, feeling her face grow warm. She didn't

realize Spud had seen something of her dismay when he com-
plimented Ruby. Hildy said quietly, "You made her feel good
about herself." Hildy turned to look at Spud. "You did a wonderful thing for her. Thank you."

Ruby stuck her head back out from inside the barn door.
"Whut's keepin' y'all? Come in so's we kin talk!"

Hildy and Spud obeyed, but things had changed, adding
more great weights to Hildy's problems.

She would ordinarily have been fascinated with learning of
how Uncle Nate had managed to get an invitation to fill the
pulpit at Thunder Mountain. Hildy wondered how he'd react
when he spoke to an empty church the first Sunday morning in
September.

Hildy's greater concern was with the startling change in Ruby's clothing and behavior. Ruby had always been the tomboy,
rough, scuffling, fighting with words or fists, and especially
directing her anger toward Spud.

That had suddenly changed. The two of them were talking
without quarreling, smiling, laughing, like real friends who
cared about each other. Yet Hildy had a secret feeling of glad-
ness: Spud was going away, but he hadn't told anyone except
her about the telegram.

Spud overheard something Nate said to Molly, so he excused
himself to Ruby and turned around. "What'd you say you're
doing to get the word out about your upcoming sermon at that
church?"

"Well," Nate explained, "I said people air goin' to their neighbors to personally invite 'em. They're a-puttin' up notices on
fence posts, bulletin boards at the local gen'ral store, things like
that. It's mostly word o' mouth 'cause they's no newspaper up
thar, an' few phones."

"How about flyers?" Spud asked. "Handbills people can pass
out? They need something they can hang on to and read and
reread; post up so they won't forget."

Ruby's jovial mood changed. "Won't do ye no good! Nothin's
a-goin' to do any good."

Her father replied gently, "You might jist be plumb su'prised,

Ruby, honey, 'cause if it's the Lord's doin', it's a-gonna git done. 'Course, I got to do my part, too. Put feet to faith, ye know."

"Good copy's what makes the difference," Spud suggested. "The right words. Something that people'll remember. So what's your uniqueness, your distinctive? Why should they come hear you?"

Ruby seemed to fret slightly that the center of interest had shifted from her. "Whut're ye a-sayin'?"

"I'm saying that this is a church so divided that even though maybe a couple hundred people live in the area, less than a couple dozen attend," Spud said. "They're so vitriolic that they've splintered the church and driven most folks away. So why should they come to hear a stranger?"

"Ye mean a sheepherder?" Nate asked soberly. "Or worse: a cowboy who sunk so low in life drinkin' and driftin' that he ended up sheepherding on a hot, empty mountainside?"

"Please don't be offended, Mr. Konning," Spud said. "I was just trying to get you—Hey!" He jumped up from the bench so fast he almost knocked it over. "That's it!"

"Whut's it?" Nate asked.

"The Shepherd of Thunder Mountain!" Spud spun excitedly to face one after another, his right hand writing invisibly on the air. "Come hear the true story of a cowboy turned sheepherder, and how his life was changed right here on this mountain! Learn how it can happen to you, too!"

Hildy felt warm tears spring to her eyes. "Oh, Spud, that's great! I'd come to hear that story."

There was general agreement. Even Ruby reluctantly agreed. "The Shepherd of Thunder Mountain shore sounds better'n preacher man. Still, I say nothin' any of us kin do's goin' to make any difference. Shore, some folk'll come to hear ye, but the fleece was fer the church to be packed. How often do ye reckon that's ever happened?"

Her father smiled weakly. "Never. I checked. That church has been thar more'n fifty years, an' it ain't never been full fer one single service." He raised his voice. "But that don't make no never-mind, neither. Ye'll see, Ruby, honey. Ye'll all see, 'cause I been doin' some powerful prayin', and lots of other good folks is a-doin' it too. Ever' night at the brush arbor, at Brother Ben's church, and 'course, at Thunder Mountain—mostly in homes there, though."

"Wish I could be there," Spud said, "but I'm heading for New York."

That announcement changed the flow of conversation, and Hildy walked outside alone. "O Lord," she whispered, "so many things are all happening at once, and I'm so mixed up!"

She felt herself start to cry, although she wasn't sure things were that bad. She stumbled rather blindly toward the pump house and collapsed on the shady side of the sagging, splintery building.

Slowly at first, then with rising intensity, the tears began to flow. "Shouldn't do this!" she scolded herself. But the tears flooded faster and faster as one problem after another flashed into her mind.

Hildy was crying her heart out when Spud found her. He didn't speak, but bent over her and looked down with eyes filled with concern.

Hildy was suddenly ashamed. "I'm sorry," she said, sniffing and rubbing the tears away with the back of her hand.

"It's all right, Hildy." He knelt and looked into her eyes. "You cry if you want."

She shook her head, making the long brown braids fly. "I've never let myself cry before. When I came home that day in the Ozarks and found my family had gone off and left me behind, I was too terrified to cry. So Ruby and I ran off from our grandmothers, looking for my family."

"I remember. That's when I met you two."

Hildy didn't seem to hear. "Then Ruby and I found them. When we were finally together again, I couldn't let my little sisters see me cry. I had to keep up their courage. I'd promised them a forever home where we'd always be together and never have to move. I couldn't let them down.

"I've been so determined to change my life, make something special of it. I've worked so hard to study and learn and plan on having a wonderful career someday. Then so many terrible things have been happening! I've been falsely accused of something I didn't do, but it could ruin everything I've dreamed about."

"Is that really why you're crying?" Spud asked gently.

Hildy's voice was weak and small and full of pain. "I don't know. That's part of it. Then Ruby found her father but they don't get along. She made him agree to a terrible fleece test that can't possibly ever be! I wonder if her father'll run off again—run from God, like Jonah, and sink deeper than he did before in his drinking and all. What'll happen to Ruby? She got so mad at her father and even me—well, she's better now, I guess, but it's not over. And if I don't clear my name, sooner or later Mr. Farnham's going to find out. Then he won't want me to work for him. I was going to use that job to start what Brother Ben said about 'purpose, plan and persevere' to get our 'forever' home."

She paused, then finished brokenly, "Now your father may be dying, and you're leaving, and I may never see you again! And Ruby looked so pretty in that dress and hat, and you and she—Oh! Why'm I crying like this?"

Hildy didn't look at Spud when he spoke, his voice low and soft and warm from a foot or so away. "You've had all those tears inside of you for a long, long time, Hildy. You needed to get that all out. Sometimes a person just needs to cry."

She heard a crack in his voice and looked up, startled. But he leaped up and turned away. "Bye, Hildy!"

She watched him almost run back toward the barn-house. Lindy jumped up from the spare shade of the roof overhang and trotted after Spud. Hildy heard the barbed wire as Spud slid through it. Then he was gone, and only the memory of him remained.

Uncle Nate and Ruby accepted Molly's invitation to stay for supper. Hildy wished they hadn't, because she was so torn up inside she could barely keep up a polite conversation. She desperately wanted to reach out, to reach up, to reach inside or wherever it was necessary to find the peace that had been able to sustain her through much of this summer's troubles.

"Let's go to the brush arbor tonight," she suggested impulsively. "Every night when I'm home, I hear the singing, and it makes me want to go. Please, Uncle Nate? Ruby?"

Her uncle smiled at her. "Since I already got my Sunday-go-to-meetin' clothes on, I reckon they'd let me in if'n I showed up with a passel o' good-lookin' women like's aroun' me now."

Hildy ran to him and impulsively gave him a big hug. She saw her stepmother looking at her in a strange way, and Hildy realized Molly had guessed she'd been crying.

Everyone looked up as a knock sounded at the barn-house door. Hildy was closest, so she opened it. A tousled-haired boy with a clip on his right pants leg straddled a relic of a bicycle.

"I'm looking for Hildy Corrigan. You her?"

"Yes," she said, feeling some apprehension at the strange boy's unexpected appearance.

"Message for you. Man gimme a dime to deliver it personal. Here."

Hildy took the white envelope with the neat return address in black, no-nonsense type: Lone River Bank.

"Mr. Farnham!" Hildy's hopes rose as she hurriedly ripped the envelope open, aware the rest of the family had gathered behind her. "Must be about the job—oh!"

The neatly typed words seemed to leap up at her. "I regret to inform you that I am removing your name from consideration as my hired girl. A matter of moral nature has been drawn to my attention, which I'm sure you already know about. Regretfully, Matthew Farnham."

Hildy's face flashed hot in shame, embarrassment and the confusion of being judged guilty without having a chance to tell her side of the story. She stood numbly while Molly removed the paper from Hildy's hands and read it aloud.

Elizabeth interrupted. "What's 'moral' mean?"

Molly said, "That means knowing the right thing and doing it. Hildy certainly knows right from wrong, but she's been unfairly accused. This case involves a watch that disappeared. Hildy didn't steal it. It's so terribly unfair of Mr. Farnham to do this!"

Nate said gently, "Maybe not from his viewpoint, him bein' a banker, I mean. Oh, I know Hildy ain't guilty, but maybe he feels he just cain't take no chances."

Hildy's whole insides seemed to be one dull ache. She said wearily, "I've got to clear my name. But how? I don't know where that watch is. I don't know if the crook stole it back, or if Mischief hid it again."

That night Hildy sat next to Ruby in the brush arbor. Ruby had said she'd go because she had a dress on, but Hildy suspected it was really because she wanted to see if the boys there would notice her. They did. Hildy saw them sneaking looks at Ruby, who smiled back at them.

Hildy kept thinking of her many problems. She felt the faintest of night breezes through the wall-less structure. During a pause between singing wonderful old comforting hymns and the strumming of the song leader's guitar, she heard countless crickets somewhere out in the dry grass.

Ruby leaned over and whispered, "Spud said he'd write me. Reckon he will?"

Hildy jerked as though she'd been stabbed by a pin.

"I didn't ask!" Ruby protested. "He done offered on his own!" She paused, then whispered, "Don't tell me he didn't say he'd write y'all?"

Hildy jumped up and dashed down the sawdust in the aisles. She fled through the open back end into the night. She stumbled across the parking lot, inch-deep dust sinking over her bare feet. She ran blindly, unseeing, toward the deepest darkness, away from the hanging kerosene lanterns in the brush arbor.

She tripped over an old tire that had been abandoned at the far edge of the parking lot. She couldn't even make out its shape in the blackness, but she recognized it by the sound and feel.

Hildy didn't bother to get up. She sat there in the dust, feeling the terrible anguish of being a victim of false accusations, of betrayal by someone very close, of a friendly world gone mad and exploding all around.

She didn't cry. There were no tears left. She withdrew inside herself until nothing existed except her pain and the blackness of the moonless night.

There was no sound of singing, no strumming of the guitar, no chorus of crickets or soft murmur of the night breeze.

What'll I do? She wasn't sure if it was a prayer or just a thought. It didn't matter. Asking the question was better than letting all the other hurts and aches chew her heart to pieces.

Suddenly she sensed rather than heard or felt something. She started to leap up, but it was too late.

A strong hand slipped around her mouth from behind. An arm grabbed her firmly about the waist and lifted her bodily into the darkness.

A muffled voice whispered hoarsely in her ear. "I'm goin' to let you down so's you can walk. You can't scream, and if you try to get away, you'll be mighty sorry!"

She was dropped back on her feet and shoved roughly toward the road leading to the barn-house. The hand stayed across her mouth so hard it hurt, and much too tight for her to make any sound through it.

"Now," the muffled voice said in a harsh whisper, "let's go get that watch!"

CHAPTER
TEN

A CLUE FROM THE PAST

H ildy tried to jerk her head free of the man's strong grip. She wanted to cry out, *I don't have the watch!* But the fingers of his right hand were too tight across her mouth.

"Hurry up!" The muffled voice was harsh in her ear.

The man stayed behind Hildy, his left arm clamped around her arm and waist so she couldn't escape. She struck backward at him with her free right hand, but he ignored her ineffective efforts. It was so dark that even if he had been in front, Hildy couldn't have made out his features.

He shoved her along, away from the brush arbor. She stumbled, her bare feet kicking up dust. In seconds, she sensed rather than saw they were approaching a car.

Hildy was having a hard time breathing, partly from fright, partly from having the man's fingers clamped so tightly across her mouth and too close to her nose. His hands smelled of something vaguely familiar, something strong and unpleasant. Hildy began to feel sick to her stomach.

"'Round the other side!" the voice growled as they neared the silhouette of the car.

Hildy felt the metal door and caught a tiny reflection from the brush-arbor lanterns on the chrome door handle.

"Open it!" the voice commanded hoarsely.

Hildy started to obey, then stopped as an idea struck her. She tried to shake her head and pushed her free right hand backward in defiance.

"You'll pay for this!" he hissed, releasing the grip with his left hand but keeping the right over her mouth so she couldn't scream.

When Hildy heard him turn the door handle, she dropped straight down like a stone. The movement was so fast and unexpected that his hand was torn from her mouth. She bit down hard on a finger as she fell. His hand seemed to nearly rip her nose up and off, but Hildy ignored the pain.

She screamed once while instantly rolling to her right in the dust. She screamed again as she scrambled away on all fours. Her captor cursed and tried to grab for her in the darkness.

Hildy screeched again and again with all the power of her lungs, tearing the night's stillness to shreds.

With another oath, the man turned away from the girl. He jerked the right door open and slid across the seat to the steering wheel. He started the car and sped off into the night.

Half sobbing with fright, Hildy jumped up and ran toward the brush arbor. She was met by Uncle Nate and others dashing to her assistance with flashlights.

Someone called the sheriff's office, and Deputy Woody Halden responded. She remembered him from their first talk after the watch was taken from Taggett's pawnshop. Hildy told the deputy everything that had happened since they last met. She included finding the watch and then having it disappear. She told about visiting Alice Quayle and her boyfriend and about the law clerk and his nasty crack. Finally, still shaken by her ordeal, Hildy was back at the barn-house.

Her father was home, so she had to repeat the story of the attack to him while they, Molly, Ruby, and Nate sat around the kitchen table.

Hildy's father listened in silence to the whole incident. Then he looked past the coal-oil lamp on the homemade table at his oldest daughter. "Well," he said thoughtfully, "at least we know the crook doesn't have the watch. But who does?"

"Mischief must have hidden it," Hildy guessed. "But that man—whoever he was—thinks I've got it, so he'll probably try again. Oh, Daddy, I'm scared!"

"Don't be," he said, reaching over and patting the back of her hand where it rested on the cracked oilcloth. "You'll be all right. The law will catch him."

"But when?" Hildy asked, trying to keep the fright and strain out of her voice. "He must've been watching me for some time. He knew I was at the brush arbor. If I hadn't walked out when I did, he'd maybe have followed us home and attacked when we were asleep. He's still out there, somewhere, watching and waiting to try again."

Another two hours passed before Uncle Nate and Cousin Ruby left. Hildy's younger siblings were all asleep. Only Hildy, her father and stepmother remained up.

"Why'd you jump up and run out from the service like you did?" Molly asked gently.

Hildy didn't want to say how she'd felt when she learned Spud had promised to write to Ruby but not to her.

Molly guessed. "It was because of Ruby, wasn't it? You were upset by the total change in her when she put on a dress, and the way Spud was nice to her when he'd never been before?"

Hildy decided to avoid a direct answer. "I'm going to miss Spud" was all she said.

Hildy's father wasn't grasping what Molly was saying. Instead, he said, "You bit that man's finger?"

"Hard. I probably drew blood."

"Then it's possible he'll have it bandaged. Since only a few people knew about the watch, maybe—"

"Oh, Joe!" Molly broke in. "Of course! Hildy, you could go see those few people who know about the watch. Learn if one of the men has a bandaged finger. Let's think who they are."

"Well," Hildy frowned, thinking. "Mr. Taggett knew about

the watch, of course, but it couldn't have been him who grabbed me."

"How about the boyfriend of the niece who pawned the watch?" Molly asked.

"Bob Medwin. But why would he—?"

"Think of reasons later," her father interrupted. "Let's just think of anyone who knew about the watch."

Hildy considered. "The lawyer, Seth Rawlins, had to know, because he handled the aunt's will. But it couldn't be Rawlins."

"How about his clerk?" Molly asked. "The one who made that nasty remark to you?"

"Merle Lamar. Yes, he'd naturally know about the map. But I can't think of anyone else."

"Didn't you say you talked to a painter next door to the lawyer's office?" her father prompted.

"Oh, I forgot. And while I was talking to him, I could hear the law clerk, Brother Ben, and Ruby through the walls."

Hildy jumped up, making the lamp rock. She reached out and steadied the base, her mind racing. "The painter! And there was some kind of a smell on the man's hand tonight when he had it over my mouth. Paint! I think I smelled paint!"

"That makes sense, Hildy!" Molly exclaimed. "Since you could hear through those walls, the painter could also have overheard anything said about the watch in the lawyer's office."

Hildy's father nodded thoughtfully. "That's three people who might be suspects. Four, if you count the lawyer. But if he knew about the picture and the map in the back of the watch, he'd have told Alice when he turned over the watch to her. Then she wouldn't have pawned it, at least not without removing the map."

"Maybe she intended to and forgot," Molly suggested.

Hildy frowned. "No, that'd be too important to forget. We're overlooking something, but I can't think what it is."

"I've got to get some sleep, because I've got a hard day's riding ahead of me," her father said with regret. "So I can't go with you to see if one of those men has a bandaged finger. And you obviously can't go alone. Maybe Nate?"

"Or Brother Ben! Being a former Texas Ranger—"

"Good idea, Hildy!" her father interrupted.

With the next step planned for Hildy to clear her name by finding the person who was after the watch, Hildy, her father, and stepmother went to bed.

Joe Corrigan left for work a little early the next morning in his borrowed car. He promised to drive by the Gilbert ranch and see if Nate could drive Hildy into town to find Ben Strong. If Nate couldn't, Joe planned to stop by Ben's place and leave a note if the old ranger wasn't home.

Because there were no telephones, Hildy could only wait throughout the morning until Nate or Brother Ben showed up or someone brought a message that neither could come.

Hildy started thinking about all the things that had been bothering her, including Spud going away as he had. To keep her mind occupied on less painful things, Hildy thought about something constructive.

"Elizabeth," she asked, "would you, Martha, and Sarah like to help me take another look to see if maybe Mischief hid that watch around here?"

The three sisters agreed. Iola was considered too young to help, so she stayed with Molly and the baby. Hildy lifted Mischief to her shoulders and made a suggestion to the girls. "Think like a raccoon. If you were Mischief, where would you hide a watch?"

With the raccoon hanging on to Hildy's braids, the search began. Hildy asked repeatedly, "Mischief, did you hide it here? Let's see."

The coon chirred contentedly, both hind legs hanging down on either side of Hildy's neck while the girl examined the barn again. The search included both living quarters and the unused side that smelled of dry old hay.

The four sisters moved on to search through the corral, now overgrown with dry summer weeds. They were careful that they didn't come across a gopher or water snake. They poked through the harness shed with its old cracked horse collars, singletrees, doubletrees, chains, and a broken spring wagon.

They even searched high places in the outhouse, carefully working so as not to disturb the wasps that nervously guarded the corners where they'd built small paper nests.

Hildy took a flashlight, handed Mischief to Elizabeth to hold, and cautiously entered the musty lower part of the gloomy two-story tank house.

It was so filled with poisonous black widow spiders that Hildy conducted that search by herself. She shivered as her fingers accidentally touched the extra strong webs. No other web felt like a black widow's. The slight disturbance caused the shiny spiders with their bulbous black bodies and distinctive red hourglass markings to start nervously toward the spot Hildy had touched. She was glad to escape unharmed.

"Nothing here," she called to the sisters through the sagging open door. "I'll check the tank."

She cautiously climbed the ladder built inside the tank house to peer through a trapdoor into the second story. The galvanized water tank glistened in the semidarkness, but there were no coon tracks in the dust.

With a discouraged sigh Hildy retreated to the sunshine. She replaced Mischief on her shoulders and led the girls to the shade of the big chinaberry tree.

Hildy looked around in frustration, trying to remember if there was some logical place they hadn't looked. She said to her sisters, "Since that man last night didn't have the watch but thought I did, that means it's got to be here somewhere." She didn't want to add her own scary thought: *He'll try to grab me again if we don't find that watch.*

Elizabeth had a very logical and practical mind. She blew light blond bangs out of her eyes and said, "There's one good thing about this. If we can't find it, that crook can't either."

Hildy looked thoughtfully at Elizabeth, remembering a strange habit. At age ten, Elizabeth was old enough to remember when there hadn't been anything to eat in the Corrigan home. She had started taking a little piece of whatever she now had to eat and hiding it. That way, if the times got that hard again, she'd always have a little something to eat. Since Mischief had become the family's only pet, the coon had learned to seek out Elizabeth's secret food cache and eat it.

"Elizabeth," Hildy said, "have we looked in every place where you've hidden food and Mischief's found it?"

"I think so. Why?"

"Maybe Mischief hid the watch in one of those places." She looked down the driveway as sunlight flashed on a car turning in by the Lombardy poplars. "Here comes Brother Ben! I hope he's coming to take me to town."

That was the reason for Ben's visit. Within an hour, he parked the big yellow Packard at the curb in front of Alice Quayle's modest frame house. A paint-splattered ladder rested against the left side of the house. Hildy followed the old ranger to the door, where he knocked.

Alice Quayle opened the door. She wore a rumpled house-dress and didn't look anything like the smart, well-dressed woman they'd first met at this house.

"Morning, Miz Quayle," Brother Ben said in his soft, easy manner. "Is Bob Bedwin around?"

"No, he's not," Alice said through the screen door. "He was helping a friend crank an old car last night. It backfired and hurt him."

Ben nodded gravely. "I got my arm broken one time doing that same thing."

"Oh, he was lucky," Alice said. "Just barely nicked him on the right forefinger."

Hildy glanced at the old ranger, who didn't let on that he understood what Hildy was thinking. Hildy quickly looked away.

He said, "Well, thanks, Miss Quayle. Nothing important. We'll catch him another time."

As Hildy and Brother Ben started to leave, Alice called out, "Oh, just a minute. I'm glad you came by. Hildy—that's your name, isn't it?"

When the girl nodded, Alice continued. "You'll be interested in this: When I was going through my late Aunt Effie's personal belongings yesterday, I found a very old letter written to her mother, my Great-aunt Clarabelle Rockwell."

Hildy frowned, not understanding.

Alice explained, "The letter was from an outlaw. That's what Bob said, and he should know, because he's interested in California history and knew the name of the outlaw, Rattlesnake Red. The outlaw was writing my great-aunt to tell her he'd robbed a stagecoach near Thunder Mountain. He was going to share some of the booty with her when it was safe to take it from where he'd hidden it. He said something about 'the Confederacy will rise again,' and they'd be ready. Isn't that the strangest thing you ever heard about?"

The old ranger smiled. "I used to hear that same expression a lot when I was young: 'the Confederacy will rise again.' I knew people who even saved Confederate money for when that would take place. But, of course, it never did."

Hildy had an exciting thought. She tried not to betray that in her voice. She asked casually, "Did Rattlesnake Red ever give your great-aunt the share he promised?"

"I don't know. That's the only letter. I'd let you see it, but Bob borrowed it."

As Hildy and the old ranger left, Hildy shared her excitement. "I think that map in the watch may be a guide to where this Rattlesnake Red hid the gold or whatever he stole from the stagecoach."

"Stages had what they called strongboxes," Brother Ben mused. "It might have survived these sixty-five or seventy years since the robbery, but everything's just guessing until that watch is found."

As they approached the lawyer's office, Hildy remembered her humiliation the last time she'd been there. She wanted to see the painter who'd befriended her before. But the painter's work was done, his ladder and dropcloths gone. A cattle buyer was moving in.

Brother Ben led the way to the lawyer's office. Hildy gulped and tried to control her feelings toward the clerk who'd been so nasty before. He wasn't in. The lawyer, Seth Rawlins, was cordial. He said his clerk, Merle Lamar, was out on an errand.

Hildy tried to sound casual as she asked, "Did you know the painter who was working next door when I first came into your office?"

"Which one? Peter Giles or Dick Archer?"

Hildy's eyebrows arched up in surprise. "There were two painters?"

"Yes. How'd you meet them?"

"I didn't exactly meet them," Hildy said evasively. "I saw one, but I didn't pay too much attention to him."

The lawyer looked over his gold-rimmed glasses. "Guess one was out for coffee or something. Don't know which one. Why? Is there something I can help you with?"

She shook her head, thanked the lawyer, and followed Brother Ben back to the Packard.

"Now what?" Hildy asked in exasperation. "We didn't get to see a single one of those men I wanted. We just know that Alice's boyfriend has a finger that might be the one I bit. But if it was really paint I smelled on the hand of the man who tried to kidnap me, then it could be the painter I saw in the office, or maybe it's the one I didn't see or even know about until just a minute ago."

"I hate to say this, Hildy, but you don't have to find the man who attacked you, because he's going to try again to get that watch. So you're still in danger."

"I know. Things keep going from bad to worse. Mr. Farnham won't hire me. Spud's left. Uncle Nate's sermon coming up. Molly's birthday is almost here, and I still don't have a present. But most of all, I've got to clear my name of these false charges. But how?"

The answer came in a most unexpected way.

—

CHAPTER ELEVEN

ANOTHER CLUE AND NEW DANGER

Hildy and the old ranger drove around awhile in the off chance they'd see painters at work. Hildy thought one of them would perhaps be able to tell where Peter Giles and Dick Archer might be. But the search was fruitless.

Half an hour later, Hildy said, "Brother Ben, could we return to the lawyer's office? I think we should tell him about being able to overhear what's said in his office. Besides, maybe his clerk's returned, so we can see if he's got a sore finger."

When the stately old gentleman again opened the lawyer's frosted-window door for Hildy, she saw the clerk seated at the front desk. His hands were out of sight in the top center drawer. He looked up and recognized the visitors.

Hildy's cheeks flushed with anger, remembering how he had treated her the first time they met.

"Mr. Lamar," she began, keeping her feelings under control and watching for his hands to come into sight, "could we see Mr. Rawlins, please?"

The law clerk removed his left hand from the desk drawer. "He went to see the judge."

Hildy realized she was holding her breath, waiting for the clerk's right hand to show. She turned to look up at the old ranger, but she continued watching the clerk out of the corner of her eye. "Could we wait, Brother Ben?"

He nodded and started to hang up his cowboy hat.

The clerk said quickly, "Mr. Rawlins may be with the judge for some time. Perhaps it'd better if you went there so he'd see you and know you were waiting."

Hildy didn't want to do that, but she also didn't want to do anything to make the clerk suspicious. She turned again to look up at the old ranger. "What do you think?" she asked.

He jerked his head slightly toward the wall separating the law office from the new cattle buyer. "Might be a good thing, Hildy."

She understood. What Hildy wanted to talk about to the lawyer definitely should not be overheard. "Let's go," she replied.

As they started out the door, Hildy turned back to the clerk. "Do you know where we might find those painters who worked next door?"

"Peter Giles is painting the outside of the judge's chambers. Maybe Dick Archer's helping. Sometimes they work together."

Hildy felt her heart speed up slightly at the possibility of talking to both painters together. She thanked the clerk and left with the old ranger.

Hildy waited until they were on the sidewalk before saying anything more. "Did you notice he never took his right hand out of that drawer?"

"I noticed. Wonder if he's got a mighty sore finger that he didn't want you to see?"

While they drove the few blocks to see the judge, Brother Ben explained that the judge's "chambers" were nothing more than an old bakery building on a corner of Lone River's side-streets. The "judge" really was a justice of the peace. He didn't have a law degree and had taught himself what he knew about law. He sold real estate to augment his meager jurist's salary.

As the Packard rounded the corner, Hildy shot an anxious glace toward the judge's chambers. "Only one painter," she said. "I recognize him. Same one I talked with in the office he was painting."

"No bandage on his fingers," the old ranger said softly as he parked the Packard under some Dutch elms. Weeds grew in the gutter and sidewalk cracks.

Hildy and Ben approached the front door where the stocky young painter was stirring paint in an open can. "Hi," Hildy said, smiling. "Remember me?"

He straightened up with a rustling of paint-splattered overalls. He adjusted the white billed cap on his head with his right hand. "Are you the girl who stumbled into the office when I was painting next to Lawyer Rawlins' office?"

"Yes. I'm Hildy Corrigan. This is my friend, Ben Strong."

"Pete Giles," he said, brushing his right palm quickly to shake hands with the old man. "Pleased to meetcha." He looked back at Hildy. "You okay now?"

"Oh yes, thanks!" She hesitated, then dived in, taking a chance. "You must have overheard what happened in the lawyer's office to upset me that day."

Pete Giles nodded. "I wanted to sock that clerk on the jaw for speaking so mean to a nice girl like you."

"Thanks," Hildy said. She looked around. "Where's your partner?"

"Dick went off somewhere. I think he said he was going to get another brush. He hates painting, so he's always finding some excuse to duck out for a few minutes."

"Dick Archer?" Hildy asked.

"Yes. You know him?"

Hildy shook her head. "No, I've just heard about him." She didn't want to arouse any suspicion, so she explained, "We're looking for the lawyer. His clerk said he was with the judge."

"They're both in there." The painter started to bend over his paint can again, then stopped. "Uh, Hildy, you're not going to tell Rawlins about what I said, are you? I mean, being able to overhear what goes on in his office?"

"I think I should, don't you, Mr. Giles?"

He sighed and slowly nodded. "I s'pose so. Uh, I overheard something else that might interest you, Hildy. It's about the watch the clerk accused you of stealing."

"Yes?" she asked, sensing exciting news.

"Well," the painter began, "one Saturday afternoon I was painting away by myself. Dick had gone home early. I heard the lawyer telling that woman, Alice Quayle, that a watch was all she'd been left."

"Go on," Hildy urged.

"I was also there early the next Monday morning, before the lawyer got in. Dick wasn't there yet, either. Anyway, I heard that clerk make a phone call. He said to the person he'd called that he—Lamar—had just discovered a codicil—whatever that is."

Brother Ben explained, "It's a supplement to a will, containing modifications or additions."

"Anyway," the painter continued, "the clerk told this guy on the phone that nobody had seen this codicil except him—not even his boss—and the codicil said there was a map hidden in the back of the watch Rawlins had given to Alice Quayle Saturday afternoon."

Hildy's heart leaped with hope. "A map?"

"Uh-huh. I didn't think much about it because it was only directions to where some stagecoach robber had hidden a strongbox he'd taken in a robbery right after the Civil War."

Hildy was so excited she could have burst, but she forced herself to sound casual. "Where . . . where did this outlaw hide the box?"

"I heard Lamar say into the phone that he didn't know, but he said that if this person on the phone could buy the watch—"

"Buy?" Hildy interrupted.

"Yes, 'buy.' Lamar said the watch'd have the map."

The painter shook his head sadly. "I figured that the clerk was just playing a joke on somebody. Anyway, I didn't want to get involved. But since I saw how upset that clerk made you, I decided to tell what I overheard."

"Thanks!" Hildy replied sincerely. "You've been a big help."

She and the old ranger left without trying to see the lawyer. Hildy could hardly contain herself. She was almost babbling as Brother Ben drove her toward home.

"It's a big break!" she said for the third time. "The law clerk was involved, but he wanted the one he called to buy the watch. But whoever the other person was didn't buy the watch. He stole it. He's the one that bumped into me and Mischief."

"Now the clerk can't say anything because he'll surely get fired for dishonesty with a client's property," Brother Ben added thoughtfully. "But whom could the clerk have called?"

"The man who stole the watch wore painters' clothes. The man who tried to kidnap me smelled of paint. And Mr. Giles said his partner, Dick Archer, didn't show up for work that Monday morning—"

"Hold on, there!" Brother Ben interrupted. "That's all circumstantial, not enough to accuse someone."

"No, but at least we now have something solid to go on! Let's try to think about what we should do now."

Hildy put aside her other concerns about Spud leaving so suddenly, the unfair fleece test that Ruby's father faced, and all Hildy's other troubles.

As the yellow Packard turned into the Corrigan driveway by the Lombardy poplars, Hildy faced the old ranger. "Let's see if I've got this straight, Brother Ben. We keep this information confidential between you and me so nobody can accidentally tip off the crook, because we don't know who he is. Right?"

"Yes, that's right."

"Then you'll see what you can learn from the painter, Peter Giles, about Dick Archer. And then we'll try to find him and talk with him."

"But not so he'll guess we consider him a suspect. Otherwise, he might do something drastic."

"You mean, like trying to grab me again to make me tell where the watch is?"

"As I said before, Hildy, you're in danger until this thing is solved and the responsible person jailed."

"I'll be careful," Hildy promised. "Thanks, Brother Ben."

Hildy got out of the car and waved as Brother Ben drove off.

The rest of the day Hildy was jumpy, looking around anxiously for any sign of danger.

She was relieved when Ruby and her father drove over late that afternoon in the ancient, topless Model T. Ruby was wearing a boy's pants and shirt instead of a dress or her usual overalls. Hildy sensed more tension between her cousin and her father.

As they walked toward the barn-house, Ruby whispered, "Hildy, I got to talk private-like to ye. Let's walk down to the river bottom."

Hildy got permission from Molly, who was already engrossed in a conversation with Nate Konning. Hildy hoisted Mischief to her shoulders and started walking down the quiet country road toward the river.

She wanted to share her day's discoveries with Ruby, but couldn't. So Hildy made small talk with her silent, withdrawn cousin until they reached the iron-trussed bridge over Lone River. They crossed the bridge and followed a narrow dirt trail down to the river bottom.

Hildy enjoyed the fragrance of willows and cottonwoods mixed with the clean, pleasant smell of the quietly flowing river. Wild grapevines crawled into the trees, draping long vines like heavy snakes back down from the lower limbs. In the distance, a hound bayed suddenly, causing Mischief to try to scramble onto the top of Hildy's head.

"Easy, Mischief!" Hildy said, gently loosening the coon's sensitive forepaws from her hair. "That's probably just Charley Jarman's old hound running loose. We won't get close, so the dog won't bother you."

"Them no-'count Jarmans!" Ruby muttered. "They still a-botherin' ye 'bout tradin' somethin' fer yore coon?"

"Haven't seen or heard them lately," Hildy replied.

The Jarmans were near neighbors to the Corrigans. Charlie Jarman was a pencil-thin coon hunter who always wore dirty overalls and heavy work shoes. He had the filthy habit of chewing and spitting tobacco. Rafe, his fifteen-year-old son, wanted to use the pet to train their coon hounds. Hildy had refused to trade, so the Jarmans had threatened to see Mischief dead, sooner or later.

Ruby cocked her head, listening. "Sounds like that ol' houn's a-comin' this way. Maybe we'uns better not take Mischief down there whar the dawg kin ketch her scent."

"I think they're far enough a way for us to be safe. You wanted to talk, so let's do that."

Mischief had been sniffing the air and hearing the river. She started to scramble down from Hildy's neck, so the girl put the coon on the ground. She promptly waddled ahead, aiming for a riffle where Hildy knew crawdads were likely to be. Mischief seemed to know that.

The girls walked along the river bottom under spreading valley oaks to the river's edge. A light evening breeze made a soothing sound in the cottonwoods. The slender willows waded at the river's edge.

"Hildy," Ruby began, picking up a small rough stick that had broken off an oak, "it ain't a-gonna work out fer muh daddy an' me."

"What?" Hildy stopped abruptly to look into her cousin's face. "What're you saying?"

"Oh, Hildy!" Ruby's voice began to rise in anguish. "I wanted to find muh daddy all these years, and now I done that, we don't git along a-tall. It's not bad enough he wants me to wear dresses and act like a lady. Now he wants me to go to that thar brush arbor ever' single night an' a reg'lar church in town on Sunday mornin'. Wants me to pray with him—family altar, he calls it—read the Bible and sech like. Ever' blessed day we git into a awful fight!

"Well, actually, I yell an' say things I'm plumb ashamed to admit. But he jist sits thar quiet-like an' says he loves me an' that's why he's a-doin' this. Hildy, I never let nobody tell me whut to do, an' I ain't a-gonna start now. I tell ye, I'm so aggravated an' put out I cain't stand it no more!"

Hildy kept an eye on her raccoon while trying to reason with her cousin. Hildy urged Ruby to be patient and try to understand her newfound father. But, as they talked, Ruby's frustration only grew worse.

Hildy was so engrossed in her cousin's problems that Mischief was forgotten in the fast-gathering dusk.

"Try to look at it from your father's viewpoint," Hildy began. "You're going to be a young woman in four or five years. You've been a tomboy, but it's time to put that behind you. That's what your father's trying to—what's that?"

She glanced around as a couple of animals growled at each other, then rolled and crashed about in the underbrush.

"Mischief?" Hildy called in sudden alarm.

Hildy couldn't see her pet in the dusk.

Ruby exclaimed, "That sounds like a houn' dawg an' a coon a-fightin'!"

Hildy's blood raced as she started running toward the sounds. "He's caught Mischief!"

"Look out!" Ruby yelled, dodging to the right.

Hildy started to jump to the left, but she was too late.

CHAPTER
TWELVE

A CHASE IN THE RIVER BOTTOM

A nearly grown redbone hound exploded from the under-brush five feet straight ahead of Hildy. She threw herself to the left, but the animal smashed into her right leg.

"Oh!" Hildy cried, falling backward into a blackberry vine.

The hound let out a startled yelp and bounded by at a full run, his right ear ripped and bloody. Hildy swiveled her head to follow him as he ran hard toward the river, tail tucked tightly between his legs.

"That's Charlie Jarman's new hound pup, isn't it?" she asked, disentangling herself from the long, vicious vines. "The one that's supposed to trail without barking like other hounds? He must've sneaked up on Mischief."

"Looks like she done whupped him good!" Ruby said with satisfaction. "Lookee how skeered that thar houn's a-runnin'. Probably won't stop 'til it's hid under Charley Jarman's front porch."

"Mischief?" Hildy called, looking around for her pet.

The coon popped out of the underbrush, chasing after the

dog in a comical, waddling run. Mischief growled deep in her throat, teeth exposed in a snarl. The little coon's fur was fully erect, making her look much bigger than she was. Her head was down to protect her throat, her back arched, her ring tail fluffed out to its fullest.

"No, Mischief!" Hildy said, ignoring the stickers from the blackberry vine. She grabbed with her right hand and caught the coon by the back of the neck. Mischief's masked face swiveled toward Hildy's hand. For a second, she thought her angry pet was going to bite. But just as the jaws opened to snap, the coon's snarl died and the mouth closed.

Hildy shoved herself out of the blackberry vines, feeling their thorns sticking and tearing her arms. Ruby took a stick and helped lift the long, clinging vines from Hildy's clothes. Ruby started laughing.

"What's so funny?" Hildy demanded, swinging the coon upon her shoulder.

"I was jist a-thinkin' how mad Charley Jarman's goin' to be when he finds out that his new houn' dawg is plumb wo'thless. Lettin' a leetle ol' thing like Mischief run him off!"

"That dog could have killed Mischief!"

"Didn't, though. Done snuck up on her, right 'nough," Ruby said. "Reckon he didn't figger on how good a fighter Mischief is. A coon kin kill a houn' if'n it's a mind to, ye know."

Hildy nodded, having heard some coon-hunting stories from her father. "The dog must have come across Mischief's scent and followed it to her. Listen, the other hound's still baying, coming this way. We'd better get out of here."

She picked the last briar from her palms just as she heard the frightened redbone leap into the river and start paddling across.

Now that it was over, the incident's funny aspects lightened the girls' cares. They both were feeling better as they hurried toward the bridge.

Hildy glanced up at the sky. "Getting dark fast. We better get out of this river bottom while we can still see enough to find the trail."

She turned around and looked back. The trees had taken on a sinister appearance. The breeze that had been a pleasant sound in the leaves now seemed to turn into a warning moan. The whole river bottom was filled with dark shadows. One seemed to move in a darting movement.

Ruby asked, "'Smatter? Ye see somethin'?"

"I guess not. Though for a second, it seemed as if something moved back there by that big old oak."

"Stop skeerin' yorself, Hildy!" Ruby warned. "Prob'bly jist some trees' shadders a-movin'. 'Sides, if they was anyone down here, it'd only be Charley Jarman er his no-count boy. All they want is fer ye to trade 'em yore coon. They wouldn't hurt ye none, I reckon."

Hildy nodded and hurried on, but she had a scary feeling that someone was following—and it wasn't the coon hunter or his son.

"Stop lookin' over yore shoulder like that!" Ruby said. "It's a-makin' me nervous. Listen! I hear the river jist ahead."

The girls made their way through the gathering darkness to stop at the riverbank. They peered around for the log on which they'd crossed, but dusk had blurred everything. Treetops in silhouette against the skyline were the only things still visible.

"Guess we'll have to wade across," Hildy said, reaching up to reassure Mischief. The coon was stirring uneasily and making little unhappy sounds. Hildy added, "See if you can tell which is the shallowest part."

The river made pleasant gurgling sounds, so the listening girls knew that water was too deep to wade safely. Hildy said, "I think it sounds shallower downstream."

"No, I think it's shall'er upstream a mite. Wait here. I'll go see."

"No, let's stay together!" Hildy exclaimed, shifting Mischief to a more comfortable position astride her neck.

"Only take a minute. Be raht back."

Hildy was annoyed, but Mischief began trying to climb up on Hildy's head. She reached up. "What's the matter with you, Mischief?" she demanded. "Why can't you just sit there?"

The coon let out a warning growl and pulled hard at Hildy's hair. Hildy automatically spun around to look behind. She took a half-step back and stopped, feeling a tangle of wild grapevines against the back of her legs.

Her mind warned: *That shadow moved! It wasn't your imagination. Mischief saw it, too.* Hildy opened her mouth to call for Ruby, but the word died on her lips.

A man's voice commanded, "Don't move!"

Through the gloom of near darkness, Hildy saw the man grab for her.

"Ruby!" Hildy shrieked, dodging aside. The shadowy man groped for her in the thickening darkness, but missed. Hildy heard him smash into some willows as he tried to keep from plunging into the river.

Hildy yelled again and spun away, the wild grapevines dangling from the trees snagging onto her clothes.

The vines! she thought. Frantically, she felt for them as the man recovered his balance and wordlessly charged her. She could only make out his moving shadow, but it was enough to tell her where he was.

"I'm a-comin', Hildy!" Ruby yelled.

Hildy reached out in the near darkness and pulled hard on a vine. *Good enough!* she thought. She grabbed on it with both hands well above her head. "Hang on, Mischief!" she whispered.

Hildy climbed hand over hand, wrapping her legs around the vine. *Sure hope this holds me*, she thought, heaving herself higher toward the lower tree branches.

She heard the man grunting below her and knew he was blindly reaching out, trying to grab her legs. Except for the first triumphant cry, he hadn't said a thing.

With Mischief complaining in sharp little agitated sounds, Hildy pulled herself up to where she bumped her shoulder against the first rough tree. She reached out quickly and felt it. *Good! Strong enough to stand on.*

She swung herself over the limb as she had often done in climbing trees with Ruby. Hildy leaned against the rough tree trunk and peered into the gloom, trying to see the limb more clearly. It seemed to extend well over the river below; maybe even all the way across.

"Got to chance it!" Hildy told herself. She started easing to her feet, holding on to higher limbs and branches.

"Hildy, whar air ye?" Ruby's voice was closer.

"Ruby, stop! Go back! I'm okay, you hear me?"

"I hear ye! Kin ye git acrost?"

"Yes!" Hildy tried to peer down into the darkness below, but she couldn't see the man. She knew he must be standing still so she wouldn't know where he was. Hildy raised her voice again. "I see the bridge. It's just about a hundred yards behind you. See if you can run up there and stop a car, find a house or somebody to help. Scream your head off, but hurry!"

"Be raht back, Hildy! I'm a-screechin'!"

For all her tomboy ways, Ruby had a young woman's high octave scream. She shredded the night with piercing shrieks of terror.

Hildy concentrated on staying out of her unknown pursuer's way. She started easing out on the limb, heading out over the river. She drew back in sudden panic, thinking a large snake's body had touched her face. Then, realizing it had to be another vine, she reached out tentatively. It dangled from above, rough and springy. She gripped it firmly and gave it a tentative tug. *Yes! I think it'll work!*

Hildy felt with her foot for where the vine sagged below her hand. *It's a long one!* she thought. She gave the vine a gentle shove with her right hand, testing. "Hang on, Mischief!" she whispered fiercely.

Hildy stood up, balancing on the rough tree limb. The solid oak did not give beneath her weight. With Mischief scolding in her sharp, shrill voice, Hildy held on to the vine and inched her feet along the limb.

She could hear the river below, swift, quiet, and dangerous. She tried to hold her breath long enough to hear where her pursuer was, but she couldn't make him out.

Now! Hildy thought as the limb began to sag under her

weight. She tugged again on the vine hanging from above. *I sure hope this works!*

She took another firmer grip on the rough, fibrous vine with both hands. She tested her weight on it. Then, satisfied, she took two quick steps and leaped into the night.

The vine sagged frighteningly under her weight as she wrapped her legs around it. For a moment she thought the vine was going to dip all the way to the river, but her momentum carried past the low point. She felt herself arching upward again.

Sure hope this vine's long enough! she thought, straining to make her extended legs reach farther toward the unseen opposite riverbank.

She glanced down fearfully and caught a quick glimpse of stars reflected in the river below. "We're past the middle, Mischief! Just a little more . . ."

Mischief complained bitterly from her perch astride Hildy's neck as the vine lost its forward momentum.

End of the line! Hildy thought, trying to see below. *Going down.*

Hildy felt her feet brush the tops of willows and knew she was on the far bank. She could barely hear the water behind and below. She strained for a little more forward motion.

Snap! The vine's breaking sounded like a pistol shot in the darkness.

Hildy fell hard, feeling Mischief pulling hard on her hair, trying to stay on the girl's shoulders.

Hildy automatically threw up her arms to protect her face. Her feet ripped through lithe willow branches that gave, slowing the girl's body to a stop while whipping her arms with stinging pain.

She plunged away from the river, breaking free of the punishing willows to collapse on solid ground. Mischief cried loudly, but was still astride Hildy's neck, pulling hard on her braids.

Hildy jumped up, listening to hear if the man had pursued her across the river. He was mouthing curses on the opposite shore.

"Thanks, Lord!" Hildy whispered.

Hildy quickly checked herself in the darkness. *Not seriously hurt*, she thought. *Scratched all to pieces, though.*

She got to her feet, steadying Mischief with both hands. She heard the man behind her wading into the river. Hildy glanced around for a light that would mark a house and safety. *Nothing!*

She tried to hold her breath and quiet her pounding heart so she could hear if her pursuer was still trying to cross the river. She could hear him in the water, cursing fiercely, but flashes of light on the disturbed water showed Hildy he had given up. He was turning back.

Hildy didn't know if he couldn't swim or if he was fearful of the swift, deep water in the darkness. It didn't matter. She had a little extra time to escape.

She looked around the darkened river bottom, aware for the first time that Ruby's screams were being answered by curious nearby residents.

One electric bulb, mounted on a wide, flat reflector, lit up on somebody's back porch on top of the riverbank. A moment later, a powerful flashlight flickered back and forth from the porch. Bright fingers of light probed the river bottom, hit Hildy's face, swept on, then darted back and held firm on her frightened face.

"Thanks, Lord!" Hildy whispered as the man with the flashlight was joined by two other men with smaller lights.

"We're coming!" one called. "Soon's I grab my gun!"

Hildy turned to look behind. Across the river, in pale scattered pockets of light, she saw a man's shadow. He was moving fast and silently away, slipping into the darkness.

Hildy sighed and waved to reassure the approaching men with their flashlights. Hildy whispered, "He's gone, but he'll be back. Next time, I may not be so lucky."

The three men who'd come to the girls' aid gave Hildy and Ruby a ride to the sheriff's office in Lone River. The deputy on duty took the girls' statements and warned them against playing in the river bottom late in the day. Another deputy drove the girls to the Corrigans' barn-house.

Hilldy's entire family and Ruby's father were terribly upset when the girls reported their adventure on the river bottom. Molly treated the girls' scrapes, cuts, and bruises with iodine. Mischief still complained in shrill little cries. Elizabeth gave the coon a small piece of hard candy she'd hidden away. Mischief took it and climbed up on a two-by-four above the girls' pallets to enjoy the treat.

The Konnings left for the Gilbert place, where they were staying. Molly instructed the four younger sisters to get ready for bed. Hildy's father motioned for her to go outside so they could talk privately.

In the night filled with the pleasant sound of countless singing crickets, Hildy's father took her by the shoulders and looked down at her. "Hildy," he began, keeping his voice low so those inside couldn't hear, "whoever's after you means business. I'm getting scared to let you out of my sight."

"He's not after me, Daddy. He's after the watch."

"Doesn't matter. He thinks you've got it, and so you're in danger until that watch is found. I think maybe you should stay at the ranch with me until this is over."

"You mean sleep in a bunkhouse miles from here? I'd die of loneliness with you gone all day, riding herd on a bunch of wild cattle. I belong here!"

"You belong where you're safe. I can't risk—"

He broke off as someone inside the barn-house let out a yell.

"That's Elizabeth!" Hildy exclaimed, turning for the barn door. Her father beat her to it.

He threw the sliding door open hard as Elizabeth squealed, "Look here! Look, look!"

CHAPTER THIRTEEN

ELIZABETH'S DISCOVERY

Hildy and her father burst through the sliding barn door. Elizabeth stood on a box in the far corner. She held something in her hand that reflected the coal-oil lamp's weak glow.

"Look!" the ten-year-old yelled again.

"The watch!" Hildy cried. "Where'd you find it?"

Elizabeth pointed toward the two-by-fours over her head. "I was hiding some cornbread in case I got hungry, and felt something behind this post. This!"

Hildy reached up quickly and took the antique gold watch with its chain from her little sister's hands. Hildy quickly examined it. "Yes, it's the same watch, all right. Mischief must have hidden it there."

Hildy's father lifted Elizabeth down. "I guess you girls never thought to look up high on the two-by-fours when you searched this place," he said.

Everyone followed Hildy to the table. She held the watch under the kerosene lamp. "Now what, Daddy?"

"I'm going to drive into town right now and turn it over to Mr. Taggett, that's what."

"He's closed," Hildy reminded him.

"We'll ask somebody where he lives, then drive by his house and give him the watch. I don't want it in this place one minute longer than necessary."

"Couldn't we at least see the lady's picture and the map first?" Elizabeth protested.

"Guess that won't hurt," her father replied.

Hildy opened the back. Clarabelle Rockwell's stern face stared out at them. Hildy wondered how she had become friends with an outlaw so long ago.

With the whole family watching, Hildy removed the picture and showed the map on the back. "See the X there behind what looks like a drawing of George Washington? That's probably where the outlaw hid the gold or treasure or whatever he stole."

"Couldn't we keep the map, even if we can't keep the watch?" Elizabeth asked wistfully.

"Wouldn't be right," Hildy explained. "Besides, Howling Cave belongs to a man named Odell Shanley. Whatever's on his property also belongs to him."

"Maybe he'd split the treasure with us," Elizabeth said. "Then we'd never be poor again."

Hildy gently replaced the photo and snapped the back shut. "We have no right to even suggest that. You see, if it hadn't been for the robber bumping into me, and Mischief somehow getting her paws on the watch, we wouldn't know anything about this treasure or whatever it is."

Molly said, "The map's part of the watch, so it belongs to Mr. Taggett."

"Or to Alice Quayle," Joe Corrigan added, "if she redeems the watch."

"What's that mean?" Elizabeth asked.

"It means that Mr. Taggett loaned money to Alice, who put up the watch as security. In case she doesn't repay the loan and redeem the watch within a certain time, Mr. Taggett can sell it. On the other hand, if Alice wants the watch back, all she has to do is repay the loan to Taggett with interest, and the watch is hers again. With the map."

Hildy added, "So, since the watch was stolen from Mr. Taggett, Daddy's going to return it to him."

"Joe, while you're there, have him call the sheriff's office, the lawyer, Alice what's-her-name, and Brother Ben," Molly suggested. "Make sure everyone knows Hildy doesn't have the watch. And Mr. Taggett should apologize for the terrible things he said about you, Hildy."

"All I want is my name cleared. Then maybe Mr. Farnham will change his mind and still hire me."

Hildy's father reached for his cowboy hat hanging on a nail by the door. "Come on, Hildy."

In Lone River, Hildy and her father stopped at a combination one-pump service station and grocery store to ask directions to Horace Taggett's home. Since Lone River was so small, everyone knew everybody else and where each person lived.

On a quiet street lined with sycamore trees, Joe Corrigan parked the borrowed car in front of a run-down house. It had a picket fence that had once been white. Father and daughter climbed the few steps and knocked.

The pawnshop owner snapped on the porch light and opened the door a crack. Before he could say anything, Hildy held up the watch.

The pawnshop owner opened the door wide and reached for the watch. "So you decided to return it, did you, you little Okie thief?"

Joe Corrigan's quick temper exploded. Both hands flashed out. He grabbed the merchant by his shirt before he could touch the watch.

"Daddy, no!" Hildy laid a restraining hand on her father's strong arm. "Please, Daddy!"

She felt him tremble with anger as he slowly released the merchant's shirt. "Mister," Joe Corrigan gritted through clenched teeth, "you don't know how close you came to getting hurt real bad!"

Taggett's eyes were wide with fear, but his attitude was unchanged. He looked eagerly at the watch as Hildy held it up in the porch light.

"Mr. Taggett, we just found this tonight. We didn't know where it was. My pet raccoon had hidden—"

The merchant's hand darted out. He snatched the watch from Hildy's hand and leaped back inside the house, slamming the door in one fast motion. The lock clicked.

Hildy's father banged on the door and shouted, "Listen, you o'nry old cuss! Hildy's tellin' the truth. You could at least thank—"

"Get offa my porch, or I'll call the police!" Taggett called through the door.

Joe Corrigan took a step back and raised his foot to kick the door. Hildy pleaded, "No, Daddy, please! Let's go to the police ourselves. Ask them to make the phone calls."

Her father was still seething when they entered the police station. It adjoined the city council chambers, where the weekly meeting was just breaking up. The police chief himself walked out, wearing casual clothes instead of his uniform.

Hildy ran up to him. "Chief Thorne, remember me?"

"The girl with the coon, right?"

She nodded. "We just returned the watch to Mr. Taggett. Please call everyone involved and tell them. You see, somebody's after me because they thought I had the watch, but I didn't. My pet raccoon did. Tonight, at the river—"

Chief Thorne stopped her. "The sheriff's office already informed me about that. Let's go into my office while you tell me about recovering the watch."

The small police station was down the hall from the council chambers. The station smelled of stale cigar smoke. A brass spittoon stood near the door. Beyond the counter on the right, there was a single cell with concrete floor and walls. The door of iron bars stood open. The cell's lone cot was occupied by a man in ragged clothes. Two other raggedy men slept on the floor.

The chief saw Hildy looking at the open door as he led them past a counter toward the back of the room. "They're not under arrest, just men down on their luck, passing through, looking for work. This Depression, you know. We let them sleep here if they want."

In the tiny, cramped office, Hildy sat on one of the sturdy wooden chairs the chief indicated. Her father took the other. The chief settled down behind a battered, cluttered desk and leaned back in a swivel chair. The protesting springs squeaked from lack of oil.

"Tell me everything," the chief said. He pulled a jackknife from the top drawer and began cleaning his fingernails.

Hildy briefly mentioned the chase on the river, which the chief already knew about. She detailed finding the watch, returning it to Mr. Taggett, and his behavior.

When she had finished, the chief stopped cleaning his fingernails. He laid the jackknife on the desk and leaned across it. "Taggett's a hard case, but I guess he's never going to change."

He reached over to a black telephone standing on his desk. He lifted the receiver with his free hand. "Now, tell me the people you want me to call."

When everyone had been phoned, the chief replaced the receiver and shoved the instrument back on his untidy desk. "Thanks for coming in, Joe, Hildy. Now you should be able to put this whole thing behind you."

"Is my name cleared now?" Hildy asked eagerly.

"There'll be some follow-up work to do, of course. But I hope we can clear your name."

On the drive out of town, Hildy was uneasy. "Daddy, what'd you suppose he meant that he *hoped* he could clear my name?"

"I guess he's just being cautious. Don't worry about it. It's over. Forget it!"

Hildy couldn't forget. She was still trying to fight an uneasy feeling when they left the city limits behind. The car's weak headlights barely punched a hole in the country darkness. The blacktopped road seemed to soak up even more of the pale light.

As they rounded a curve, Joe Corrigan suddenly jerked the wheel hard to the left and slammed on the brakes. Hildy had a glimpse of a large, dark-colored car on the right side of the road, not quite on the shoulder.

"Crazy fool!" Hildy's father exclaimed, whipping the wheel over hard to the right and crossing back into his proper lane again. "Parking on the road like that."

He stopped, jerked the hand brake back hard, left the lights on, and jumped out onto the road. Hildy called, "Don't lose your temper again."

The lone occupant of the other car hurried to meet Joe. Hildy heard a man's voice say, "Thanks for stopping, mister. My car just died so sudden-like I couldn't even get it all the way off the road. Ran out of gas."

Joe Corrigan's half-running steps slowed. Hildy suspected the quick explanation had softened his anger. She leaped out and ran back toward the two men in case her father was still fighting mad.

Joe Corrigan said tersely, "I almost hit you, coming around that curve. You better turn your lights on before somebody comes along."

"You're right, mister. Just a minute."

Hildy stood by her father at the front of the long vehicle when the head lamps came on. The girl turned her head away until the lights were dimmed. She glanced at the manufacturer's insignia on the front.

"Looks like an Uncle Sam's hat in a ring," she said to her father. "What kind of a car is it?"

The stranger walked back to the front in time to hear Hildy's question. "Rickenbacker. Straight eight. Too much car for me. I can't afford to run it. I'd like to park it right here and never come back."

Hildy sensed her father's sudden interest. Knowing he needed a car and that he'd soon have to return the borrowed one, she felt her own interest rise.

Joe Corrigan said casually, "Be hard to get anybody to take a car like this off your hands." He sauntered around to the left side of the long vehicle.

Hildy recognized her father's opening words when he was going to try bargaining for something. She'd been with him before when he'd traded for horses and one car.

"Oh, it's really a great car!" the stranded driver assured him. "It's as long a one as was ever made. Family sedan, though, not for a bachelor like me."

"Probably a gas guzzler," Hildy's father commented as he peered into the backseat.

"You're sure right there, mister. Two carburetors. That's why I'm stranded out here in the country."

"The pistons probably say to each other, 'You take this gallon, and I'll take the next.' You probably can't pass a gas station without stopping."

"You musta owned one of these babies," the man said. "Manufactured by Eddie Rickenbacker, the American air ace of the Great War."

"Never saw one before," Joe Corrigan said, walking past around to the spare tire mounted on the rear.

Hildy stayed with the two men as they continued on the right side, past the other running board to the front again. Hildy sensed that the stranger guessed her father was interested in the car. She couldn't figure out why her father was even talking about a car that took so much gasoline. But she suspected he had something in mind to beat the gas problem.

"My name's Fred Menton," the stranger said.

"Joe Corrigan. This's my daughter Hildy."

The men shook hands, and Fred tipped his cap to Hildy. Through the reflected light of the head lamps, she saw he was in his twenties. He wore casual pants, a short-sleeved shirt and a tie.

"Family man, huh, Joe?"

"Five girls and a boy."

"This'd make a great car for them," Fred said. "Lots of room. And it's got two of everything, including dual ignition. Four cylinders to each ignition."

Hildy's father shook his head. "I'll bet, in setting the timing, you'd have to time each ignition to synchronize with the other."

"You're right, Joe. You must be a mechanic?"

"Shade-tree mechanic," he admitted. "You must get about five miles to a gallon of gas."

"Right again, Joe. But otherwise, this is a great car. I've got another, a 1928 Chevrolet, but it needs repairs. It's so box-like it doesn't impress the girls much compared to this Rickenbacker, but I just can't afford this one. Say, how about this? I'll swap you repairs on my Chevy for the Rickenbacker. Good mechanic like you can have a great family sedan."

"I don't know, a gas hog like this—"

"Give me a ride home and let's talk."

On the drive back into town, Hildy vainly tried to guess her father's reason for continuing to show cautious interest in the gas-guzzling sedan.

When they dropped Fred off at his parents' house, Joe said, "I'd like to swap, but I've got no time. I work sunup to sundown six days a week."

"That's no problem, Joe! I got electric lights in my garage. You could work an hour or so each night."

"Well, I suppose that's possible."

"Great! Tell you what, Joe. Gimme a dollar earnest money to seal the deal now, and I'll give you a bill of sale. Then tomorrow night we'll sign the other papers."

Hildy knew it was too far past payday for her father to have a dollar left. She also knew he didn't want to be embarrassed by admitting that.

Hildy motioned for him to bend down. She whispered, "You can have my sixty-five cents."

"That's for Molly's birthday present."

"It's not enough to buy her anything, so I'll make her something."

"Thanks anyway, Hildy." He straightened up. "Fred, I'll give you two bits tonight as earnest money, and the rest tomorrow. Fair enough?" He pulled out a quarter. Fred took it, produced a pen and wrote a bill of sale.

As the Corrigans turned to leave, Fred said, "Listen, Joe, in this Depression a family man can always use a little extra cash. Tomorrow night when we finish the paper work on this car, I'll tell you how to make maybe five, ten dollars."

"Yeah? How?"

"Selling watermelons."

"I don't have any melons, or money to buy them."

"Don't need any. They're free, rotting in the fields near here. Friend owns them, so I'll tell you where they are. You and your girl can load up the Rickenbacker with them, park by the road-side, and sell them for maybe a dime or quarter apiece. Deal?"

Hildy held her breath, thinking, "Maybe Daddy'll give me a little money for helping! Then I can buy a nice birthday present for Molly!"

Her father gripped the younger man's hand again and said, "Deal."

On the drive home, Hildy tried vainly to get her father to say why he'd bought the Rickenbacker. He just grinned and said, "Wait a few days, and I'll show you a trick with a hole in it." It was an expression he used when he didn't want to tell any more.

Hildy shrugged, her mind jumping to other matters. *Well, now that the watch's been returned, things should get better*, she thought. She tried to believe that, but something inside warned, *This isn't over yet, not nearly over!*

CHAPTER
FOURTEEN

A STRANGE REPORT

The next day Hildy helped Molly around the barn-house. School would start in a little more than three weeks, and the family had to make all the girls' clothes. Only shoes would be bought.

Hildy gently pushed Mischief from where she was trying to taste the fabric for Elizabeth's new dress. "I know coons eat almost everything," Hildy scolded, "but leave the dress for Elizabeth." The coon went off to check on an empty spool that had rolled under the table where Hildy worked.

Hildy's fingers returned to sewing a button on the garment, while her mind wandered off. *Wonder how far Spud's hitchhiked by now? Why didn't he offer to write me as he did to Ruby? He sure acted different around her when she wore that dress! Wonder if she and her father are getting along any better? Too bad about the fleece test. I just hope a few people show up to hear Uncle Nate preach at Thunder Mountain.*

Molly asked, "What're you thinking about?"

Hildy bit off the thread and held the dress up to check it. "Oh, lots of things."

"Like why your father traded for that gas-eating car?"

"That, and other things."

"Like Spud?"

Hildy felt a surge of emotion. She reached out and smoothed some cloths on the end of the table. A piece of an old sheet had been placed over the cloths to make an ironing board.

"I wonder how far he's hitchhiked toward New York." Hildy drew the new dress over the makeshift ironing board and smoothed out the wrinkles. She switched the subject. "And I wonder why Mr. Taggett was so mean to me when I returned the watch."

She headed for the hot kitchen stove, saying, "And how can I get into town to see Mr. Farnham? I hope he'll change his mind and let me work for him. I need that job to start saving money for college."

"I'm sure the banker's heard by now how you cleared your name."

Hildy stood over the wood-burning stove with the two flatirons on the top burners. "I keep thinking about what the chief of police said. I had a funny feeling he wasn't quite sure I'd proved my innocence."

Hildy picked up the curved handle and pressed the bottom part against the grooves in the top of the hot iron. They clicked firmly into place. She lifted the iron and returned to the table.

Elizabeth looked up from where she was changing the baby's diaper. It had been made from an old fifty-pound flour sack. "Car coming!" Elizabeth said.

The three younger sisters ran to the door and peered through the cracks. "Policeman!" Martha announced.

Hildy's heart jumped, and a ripple of fear passed over her body. Then she relaxed, knowing that Mr. Taggett now had his watch back. Hildy quickly returned the hot flatiron to the stove and hurried to the barn door.

Deputy Woody Halden's boots kicked up little puffs of dust as he crossed the bare yard to where Hildy, Molly and the other sisters were waiting. He accepted Molly's invitation to come in. He sat on the bench by the table while Elizabeth brought him a glass of water in a tin cup. That was all the refreshment they could offer. He took a sip, then set the cup on the cracked oil-cloth.

"You folks won't believe what happened last night," he said soberly.

"Tell us!" Elizabeth urged.

Hildy wanted to echo that, but she kept quiet while the rest of the family took seats around the table and looked expectantly at the visitor. He looked directly at Hildy.

"You and your father returned the missing watch to Horace Taggett at his home last night. Right?"

Hildy nodded, sensing something was very wrong.

"I talked to the police chief this morning. He told me about your having him make all those phone calls. Guess one of those people wanted the watch enough that he burglarized Taggett's place some time after midnight."

"What?" Hildy cried.

The deputy nodded. "Taggett left the watch in plain sight on his dresser. He said he's such a heavy sleeper he didn't hear a thing. But when he got up this morning, the watch was gone."

Hildy moaned. She could see her name again being dragged through the dirt of doubt and suspicion. "The watch was gone?"

"Yes and no. The watch was taken in the burglary, but Taggett found it just outside the house this morning."

"Oh-oh!" Hildy muttered. She could already guess the rest.

"What's that mean?" the deputy asked sharply.

Hildy gulped twice before asking, "Was the watch open when it was found?"

The deputy squinted thoughtfully at her. "Yes, it was. Taggett told the police that the back end was open when he picked it up near his backyard gate."

"Was there anything in it?" Hildy asked in a quavering voice.

"I don't think so. No, I'm sure I'd have been told if there was something there." He cocked his head and looked at Hildy with narrowing eyes. "What was supposed to be in the back of that watch?"

Five-year-old Sarah piped up, "A lady's picture. I saw it. She had funny hair! Like this." She demonstrated a part in the middle and a bun on the back.

The officer smiled at the little towhead. "Well, I guess if only a picture's missing, there's no great loss. But this case has taken so many twists and turns that it's making both the sheriff and police chief mighty nervous. So they would like you to tell me anything that might be helpful in figuring out what's going on with this watch."

Hildy started to answer, but stopped upon catching a warning look from her stepmother.

"Your father'll be home shortly, Hildy," Molly said softly. "Why don't you wait for him while you try to think if there's anything else you should tell the officer?"

Hildy nodded and said goodbye to the deputy. When he had gone, Hildy turned to her stepmother. "Why didn't you want me to tell him about the map?"

"I feel we should talk this over with your father first. I'm concerned for your safety, so I think we'll just wait until he gets home."

Hildy returned to her ironing while suggesting the younger sisters go out to play. When they were gone, Hildy turned to her stepmother. "I don't know who took the watch and dropped it after taking the picture, but I do know why. Someone wants that map. I just can't figure out who. Obviously not Mr. Taggett. The only other persons who knew where the watch had been returned were the ones the police chief phoned when Daddy and I were in his office."

"That'd be the woman who pawned the watch, the lawyer, and Brother Ben. He certainly didn't do it!"

"No, but Alice could have told someone, or the lawyer, Mr. Rawlins," Hildy suggested.

Molly jabbed a pin into the cushion. "Well, Hildy, I hope I'm wrong, but I wouldn't be surprised if Mr. Taggett again tries to blame you for somehow being involved in last night's burglary."

"That's exactly what I was thinking. But this time I can protect myself."

"How?"

"Whoever took the picture with the map is going to try getting into Howling Cave to see if he can find whatever's hidden there. The owner, Mr. Shanley, has the entrance barred, but if someone really wanted to break into the cave, he could. So Mr. Shanley needs to be warned."

"Let the sheriff do that. No need for you to go up there, even if you had a ride."

"That sounds logical, Molly. But let's check it with Daddy when he gets home."

Joe Corrigan arrived early because he wanted to complete the deal for the Rickenbacker. Molly sent the younger children outside to play again. They had been running in and out all afternoon. She made a quick supper for her husband. He listened to Hildy's account of the deputy's visit. Then he used a piece of biscuit to sop up the last of the country gravy with red beans.

"I'll stop by the police station or the sheriff's office and tell them about the map," he said. "Let them warn the cave owner. You want to ride with me, Hildy?"

On the drive to town, her father finally explained why he had traded for the Rickenbacker. "I can't afford gas for the car, so I'm going to replace the gasoline tank with one that'll burn stove oil. It only costs three cents a gallon. There's no road tax on stove oil. It's exempt, like tractor fuel."

"Will stove oil burn in a car?"

"It will in the Rickenbacker because the ignitions are so hot. Some people are mixing gasoline with stove oil to start. Service stations say you have to have your own drum, because it's against the law to put stove oil in a gas tank. But I'll buy my own drum and get the stove oil from the truck driver who delivers it. Then I'll remove the Rickenbacker's gas tank and install one for oil. All perfectly legal."

Hildy gave him a quick hug. "You're the smartest daddy in the whole world!"

"We'll see about that after I finish the deal with Fred and find out the details on those watermelons. Say, since I'm working, how would you like to help sell the melons and make a little money to buy Molly's birthday present?"

"Would I?!"

"How about a dime on each dollar's worth sold?"

She gave him another hug. "Let's see? My share would be a dollar for each ten dollars sold, less the tithe."

Hildy always put aside ten percent of anything she earned as the Lord's. She continued. "If Elizabeth and Martha helped, I'd have to give them something."

"I'll take care of them."

"Thanks! So if I had ninety cents plus the sixty-five cents I've already got, I can get Molly something nice. But you know, Dad, I'd still like to give her that watch. Did you notice how her eyes lit up when she looked at it and touched it?"

"Yes, but there's no way we can sell enough melons to buy that watch. I just hope they catch the guy who stole the map so this whole mess can be forgotten."

When the legal transfer papers were signed and the amount of labor determined, Joe drove Fred to where the Rickenbacker had broken down. They poured five gallons of gas into its tank. Fred drove the Rickenbacker to the Corrigans', where Joe left the borrowed car. Hildy and her father rode with Fred in the Rickenbacker to his place while he explained about the free watermelons and how to find them.

Hildy and her father waved goodbye to Fred; then they drove down the paved state highway to Tuttlesville, an agricultural town twenty miles away. By then, Hildy's father was already looking for a service station.

He traded the Rickenbacker's spare tire for half a tank of gas. As the attendant filled it, Hildy walked over to a billboard sign. It read:

NO JOBS IN THIS TOWN!
WE CAN BARELY TAKE CARE OF OUR OWN!
PLEASE KEEP GOING.
TUTTLESVILLE CHAMBER OF COMMERCE.

It had been five years since the Crash of 1929 when the Depression started. After a year in office, President Roosevelt used his Fireside Chats to encourage Americans to believe things were improving. The Corrigan family saw no signs of that, but Joe was a Roosevelt man.

The minute the Rickenbacker turned off the paved highway onto the city's main, unpaved streets, the sedan slowed noticeably. Hildy leaned forward to stare through the windshield. "What's that?"

"Sand! Road's so sandy they've thrown straw on it so wagons and cars can get through. Fred was right when he said growers couldn't get their melons to market. The wagons sink in the sand, and the teams can't pull the load. No wonder they're giving melons away."

Hildy leaned out the window. "I can't believe the main street's like this, Daddy!" She pulled her head back in. "Are we going to be able to make it through?"

"Lots of power under this hood. We'll make it there because of the straw. I'm not sure how we'll do when we head home on sandy country roads with a load of melons."

Darkness had settled when they found the ranch Fred had told them about. The grower was a big man in overalls with heavy, scaly hands. "Yust take all da melons you vant," he said with a lilting Swedish accent. "You von't even haf to go into da field."

He walked into the driveway, which was illuminated by a single large bare bulb mounted on a reflector atop a pole in the barnyard. "My son overloaded da vagon an' got stuck in da sand. He cuss and he yell, but da mules couldn't pull it out. So he put dry tumbleveeds under dem an' set da veeds afire."

"Oh, no!" Hildy exclaimed. "Those poor mules!"

The old grower chuckled. "Not poor mules. Poor vagon! Mules yust moved enough to set it on fire. My son threw sand an' put it out. He unhitched da team an' came home. Melons is still dere in da vagon. Take all you vant!"

Hildy and her father found the scorched wagon. The melons were in good shape but covered with fine sand. They could wash the sand off.

Hildy and her father transferred as many melons to the big

Rickenbacker as Joe Corrigan considered safe. Then he eased the sedan out of the sandy road. They slowly made their way back to the paved highway. From there they drove home to the barn-house.

There a shock was waiting for Hildy.

CHAPTER
FIFTEEN
—
WORD FROM SPUD

I t was late when the Rickenbacker stopped before the barn-house. Hildy had expected everyone except Molly to be asleep. Instead, as Hildy picked up a sandy watermelon to carry inside, Elizabeth's towhead popped through the barn door when Molly slid it open.

"Hildy!" Elizabeth shrieked, dashing across the dusty yard. "A letter came for you! From Spud!"

"From Spud? Where is it?"

"Shh," Molly cautioned, laying her right forefinger across Elizabeth's lips. "You'll wake the kids."

"On the table." Elizabeth raced back toward the barn door. Hildy ran awkwardly behind, holding the melon.

"Here!" Elizabeth snatched the envelope from where it leaned against the base of the coal-oil lamp.

Hildy almost dropped the melon onto the floor in her hurry. She quickly brushed the sand off her hands and grabbed the envelope. Then she frowned. "There's no stamp and no post-mark." She looked at Molly and Elizabeth. "And there's no rural free delivery out here. So how'd you get this?"

"A man delivered it," Molly explained. "He said—well, you'd

better read it. Then I'll tell you."

Hildy tore the envelope open with shaking hands. She gulped as she saw the familiar handwriting. Yet it didn't look quite the same, somehow. She silently skimmed the words: *Dear Hildy. I was stricken with some mysterious malady . . .* "Oh no!" Hildy exclaimed aloud.

"What's the matter?" Elizabeth asked.

Molly said, "Finish the letter!"

Hildy continued reading with dread, suddenly understanding why the handwriting was unsteady and irregular. . . . *mysterious malady that left me weak as a kitten. Fortuitously, this occurred near Thunder Mountain, so the man who was giving me a ride took me to Mrs. Benton's place. . . .*

Hildy read faster, her eyes picking out key words and phrases, *. . . incredibly ill . . . might have died . . . no physician. . . . Mrs. B. nursed me. . . . I'm improving . . . still too weak to travel, Mrs. B declares.*

With rising excitement and concern, Hildy's eyes raced on. *The kids and I have mapped a strategy to help Ruby's father at least have a few people attend his upcoming sermon. . . . Maybe I'll still be here. . . . Hope to see you . . .* Hildy's heart jumped; then her eyes saw the words *. . . and Ruby.*

Hildy sat down weakly on the bench, the letter in her lap, her mind spinning. She barely heard Molly's explanation of how the letter had arrived. One of Mrs. Benton's neighbors had stopped by. Spud's letter had been given to him with the promise he'd pass it on to someone at the nearby small grocery store. In turn, someone driving down from Thunder Mountain had carried the letter to the Corrigans' barn-house.

Hildy had terribly mixed emotions. *Is Spud all right? I'd like to see him! Will he still be there when we go up to hear Uncle Nate preach his fleece sermon? Has Spud also written to his parents about his delay? Will his father still be alive when Spud gets there?*

Then Hildy's mind jumped. *What about Ruby? Did Spud write her too? I've got to find out.*

It was too late to ask her father to drive over to the Gilberts', where Ruby and her father were staying. Hildy had no choice but to wait until morning.

She discussed Spud's letter with her father and stepmother. Elizabeth went to bed, satisfied with having stayed up to find out what the letter said. Hildy helped her father unload the melons in the west side of the barn and sweep out the sand from the Rickenbacker.

Her father said, "There's not much traffic on this country road, Hildy, but maybe you could set up a stand by the end of our driveway. See if you can sell any melons. Maybe I can get home early again tomorrow. We can drive closer to town and try selling out of my new car."

Hildy agreed, then washed her feet and crawled onto the bedding pallet with her sisters. The two younger ones slept at the foot of the bed between Hildy and Elizabeth. Hildy ignored Martha's toenails and prayed silently but earnestly for Spud's safety. Then she slept.

She dreamed weird, mixed-up things. Mr. Taggett showed up with Deputy Halden, yelling, "Arrest her! She helped steal the picture from my watch! Little Okie thief!"

The dream twisted and changed. Spud looked up weakly from the dirt floor in the dugout where Mrs. Benton held a damp cloth to his fevered brow. "Oh, hi, Hildy. I was expecting Ruby."

The dream shifted again. Hildy was in Howling Cave, but she was alone. Her flashlight made shadows leap from President Washington's silent stone face. She looked for the X just as her light went out. In the sudden, total darkness, she heard a foot-step behind her.

In the crazy way of dreams, she was in Brother Ben's big yellow Packard as he drove. Hildy leaned forward to see the glistening white church ahead. A big sign over the front porch read:

TODAY!
SHEPHERD OF THUNDER MOUNTAIN!
ALL WELCOME!

But there wasn't a single car, buggy or wagon in sight. Nobody had come.

Ruby in boy's overalls gloated before her stricken father.

"See? Yore not s'posed to be no preacher man! An' I don't have to wear dresses, neither!"

Spud reappeared in Hildy's dream. He said to Ruby, "I like you in a dress."

She smiled at him. "Ye do? I'll go change raht now!"

Mr. Taggett also reappeared, smiling and showing Hildy the watch. She said, "It's perfect for Molly's birthday."

The watch suddenly vanished. Taggett's smile also vanished. He turned to the police chief. "Arrest her! She stole my watch—again."

"No!" she protested. "My name'll be ruined. Mr. Farnham won't hire me. I'll never go to college. I'll never get our forever home!"

"I don't care, you Okie gal!" Taggett's finger waggled in her face. "You're going to jail!"

"No!" she cried, striking out at the terrible images. "No!"

"Hildy, wake up!" Molly whispered hoarsely.

Hildy opened her eyes, her heart pounding. The first hint of daylight was showing in the cracks and the window on the eastern wall of the barn-house. She gave a long, shuddering sigh of relief and got up.

Her father had already left for work in the Rickenbacker. Hildy asked Molly for any suggestions on how to get to see Ruby. It was too far to walk, and there was no phone. "You'll just have to wait, Hildy," her stepmother counseled.

"Guess so. While I do, maybe I can sell some melons."

While Mischief looked on, Hildy made two three-foot-square signs on old pieces of carboard boxes turned inside out. With an indelible pencil she wrote in letters six inches high:

ANY WATERMELON 10 CENTS.

She filled in both numbers so they were an inch wide. Then she wet all the letters so they glistened with purple permanency.

She cut gunnysacks open along the seams and tacked them across two-by-fours crudely nailed to make a square. She hammered triangle braces at the bottom so the squares would stand. The raccoon played with the nails, chirring happily.

"Molly," Hildy said, "there's one advantage in being the oldest child in a family with only one boy, and him only fifteen months old."

Hildy laid down her hammer and stepped back to admire her work. "There, that'll help keep the sun off."

When her sisters were awake, they helped wash the sand off the melons. Mischief played in the water, leaving almost-baby-like footprints everywhere. The coon ambled along as the two older girls carried melons and signs to the county road by the Lombardy poplars. Molly didn't feel it was safe for three-year-old Iola to be away from the barn-house.

Elizabeth and Martha struggled at either end of a kitchen bench they carried down the long, dusty lane. Mischief insisted on riding in the middle, swaying precariously from time to time as the bench threatened to tip over. The girls placed it in the Bermuda grass on the shoulder beside the main road. Mischief jumped off, complaining because the ride was over.

Hildy dragged the sack screen to the road and propped it up. The bench was placed well in front of the screen so anyone on the road had an unobstructed view of it. When there were no customers, the screen would shelter the girls from the fierce August sun.

Hildy used a bread knife to cut a triangle plug from a twenty-pound melon. "Umm! Perfect!" she exclaimed, chewing the sweet, juicy piece. Hildy cut the melon in half and carefully set both glistening red sections on the bench. Each piece faced a different direction. People coming down the road from east or west would see the melon from a distance and have time to stop.

She gave thin slices of the melon's heart to her sisters and one to Mischief. The coon liked that sample so much the girls had to take turns holding Mischief to keep her from from eating the whole melon.

"Here comes someone!" Elizabeth exclaimed as the girls stood back to admire their work.

A perspiring man in faded blue overalls and matching shirt pulled back on the reins of a brown mule. The flat wagon stopped by the girls. Hildy saw a plow with a shiny blade lying on the wagon's back end.

"Nice-looking coon you got there," the man said by way of greeting. He tossed the lines around the brake handle and sauntered to the bench. He smelled of old sweat and dust. Sarah's nose wrinkled, but the man didn't notice. "How about a taste?" he asked.

Hildy sliced a thin section out of the melon's center. She watched anxiously as he chewed with his mouth open. Red juice dribbled unheeded down his whiskery chin. Hildy lowered her eyes and Sarah turned away.

"Hmm," the prospective buyer mused. "Not quite ripe." When Hildy stared in silent disbelief at the obvious untruth, the man suggested, "Maybe another bite or two could show I'm wrong."

Hildy took the hint, but when the man reached for a fourth piece, she shook her head. "You've had enough samples to make a choice, I believe."

"I do believe you're right, little lady." He looked up the long lane toward the barn-house. "How about I plow you a garden? Ten melons for one hour."

Hildy shook her head, the brown braids flopping emphatically. "Cash and carry," she said.

The man looked longingly at the remaining piece of melon, then wiped his mouth with the back of a grimy hand. "Didn't bring my pocketbook." He turned back to the wagon and loosened the lines from the brake handle. "Maybe some other time, girls."

Hildy, Elizabeth and Martha stood in fuming disbelief as the wagon rattled away on iron-bound wheels.

Practical Elizabeth said, "He did that on purpose! Didn't intend to buy at all. Well, we won't let that happen again, will we, Hildy? One bite's enough!"

Hildy agreed. When an Oakland car rattled down the road and slowed to a stop, the girls announced their one-free-bite rule. The burly driver took a single bite and smacked his lips. "Ten cents each, huh? How about three for a quarter?"

Hildy and Elizabeth exchanged glances. The ten-year-old shook her towhead. "Seven for four bits," she said. She was showing off her knowledge of the California term for a half-dollar. She added, "That's what we think's fair, don't we, Hildy?"

Hildy tried to smile at her sister's level-headed logic. "That's right, mister."

"What'll I do with seven melons?" the driver protested.

Elizabeth replied instantly. "Be nice to give some to your neighbors, or your pastor if you go to church."

The man grinned. "You gals are going to do all right in this world." He reached into his pants pocket and produced a coin. "Here's your money—if that includes helping me load the melons in my car?"

"It does," Hildy replied with a happy grin.

By noon, when the sun was high and the gunnysack screen was useless, the girls took turns going to the barn-house for lunch. Elizabeth and Sarah went first, taking the raccoon with them. Hildy and Martha stayed to watch the stand.

Hildy counted the coins in a silvery tin cup. "Ninety cents," she announced with satisfaction. "If we keep at this until all the melons are gone, we're all going to have money. I'll pay my tithe and buy Molly's birthday present with my share."

Martha looked to the east as an old topless Model T Ford came chugging down the road. "Looks like Uncle Nate's car! Yes, it is. I see Ruby in the front seat."

Hildy shaded her eyes with her hands. "You're right." She thought of her dream, and wondered if Spud had also written her cousin of his illness. Then Hildy frowned and added, "From the way Uncle Nate's driving, something must be wrong!"

Hildy and Martha took a few steps toward the approaching Model T. It came to a shuddering stop, sending up a cloud of dust that covered the cut melon with a fine, gritty mist.

Ruby leaped out of the car in her boy's overalls. Her hazel eyes were wide and her face flushed. "Hildy, that thar depity was jist at our place a-lookin' fer ye! That mean ol' Mr. Taggett was with him, and he was *mad*!"

"Mad?" Hildy cried. "Why?"

"They air a-comin' to arrest ye!" Ruby blurted.

CHAPTER

SIXTEEN

STARTLING NEWS

A rrest me? Why?" Hildy asked.

"'Cause Mr. Taggett's so blamed mad he was practic'ly spittin' nails when he was at our place!"

Hildy turned to her uncle. "What'd he say?"

Nate Konning put a long arm around Hildy's thin shoulders. "Near's I could make out, yestidy that thar gal, Alice, come in Taggett's place to redeem her watch. Paid cash. When he handed it over, she opened the back and let out a squall. Said Taggett'd stolen her great-aunt's pi'tcher, an' she wanted it back raht then!"

Ruby broke in. "The depity said Alice made sech a to-do about Taggett a-stealin' her prop'ity that they done had to call the po-lice. The chief, he come to the store and 'splained to Alice that somebody's broke in Mr. Taggett's home after ye returned the watch. Took the pi'tcher and left the watch in the backyard. But Alice didn't believe him. She screamed and hollered so loud at Mr. Taggett that he got mad and started a-yellin' back. Said it was all yore fault, Hildy! So he went to see the judge and then he called the sheriff's office. Then the depity and ol' Mr. Taggett come a-ridin' out to our place."

Hildy shook her head. "That doesn't make sense! Why would they look for me at your place?"

Uncle Nate patted Hildy's shoulder. "I got me a sneakin' suspicion that Taggett done made the depity mad, and he misled Taggett. It's plain as the nose on yore face that thar depity don't cotton much to that thar loudmouthed Taggett. Wouldn't be su'prised none if the depity likes you a whole lot better, Hildy.

"Anyways, I figgered the depity told Taggett you was likely to be at yore cousin's. Then when they left, a-headin' thisaway, I seen their car off'n the road with both sides of the hood raised."

Ruby added, "We'uns figgered the depity done that a-purpose, that he didn't really have no car trouble a-tall. But it give us a chanct to drive here real fast an' warn ye."

Hildy took a quick breath, trying to think. "Thanks, but there's nothing I can do except wait until they come."

"They'll drag ye off to jail!" Ruby warned. "Why don'tcha take shanks mare acrost the fields? Hide out in the river bottom 'til that o'nry old Taggett cools off?"

Hildy shook her head emphatically. "I can't do that!"

Her mind whirled like a windmill in a storm. She was aware that Ruby and her father didn't seem so tense today. Maybe it was because they were getting along better, Hildy decided. She hoped so.

Hildy helped Martha load the melons into the backseat floorboards of Uncle Nate's borrowed Model T. The sisters rode in the backseat of the topless vehicle to the barn-house, which was filled with the aroma of freshly baked biscuits and red bean soup. Molly was told what was happening.

"Even though I've got nothing to do with all this, Mr. Taggett's going to drag my name through the mud again!" Hildy said. "I'm not guilty, but some people are not going to believe that. Like Mr. Farnham. He'll hear about it and never change his mind about hiring me!"

Elizabeth kept an eye to a crack in the barn door to announce when the deputy's car arrived. Hildy, Ruby, and the adults waited anxiously for the two men.

Five-year-old Sarah didn't understand her older sister's concern, so she tried to change the subject. "Hildy got a letter," she announced solemnly to Ruby. "From Spud."

Ruby turned to look at Hildy. "Ye did? Air he back in New York a'ready?"

Hildy shook her head and suppressed a sigh of relief. Obviously, Spud hadn't written Ruby. So, in spite of her own problems, Hildy felt good about that. She handed Spud's letter to Ruby, who read it slowly, her lips moving as she sounded out the words in a silent reading.

Ruby handed the letter back to Hildy just as Elizabeth called from the door, "Here they come!"

Molly hurriedly sent the four younger girls outside to play. The uniformed deputy and the heavyset merchant in a baggy suit took seats on the only remaining bench by the table.

"Miz Corrigan, I'm sorry to come out here at mealtime," the deputy said. "But this won't take long."

Taggett's face was flushed to his bald scalp, but he remained silent while Deputy Woody Halden told everyone what Ruby and her father had moments before relayed to the Corrigans.

The deputy finished and looked at Hildy. "So Horace here—and everyone else—now knows about the missing map on the back of the woman's picture."

Hildy wondered briefly if the deputy's use of the merchant's first name was intended to lower his importance. Hildy thought, *At any rate, a person just doesn't rate as high up when he's not called mister or missus.*

As if to confirm her thoughts, the deputy added, "Hildy, Horace wants to press charges against you for conspiracy to steal the picture."

She started to protest her innocence, but the officer held up his hand and stopped her. He added, "Horace talked to the judge, and he told him there's nothing but circumstantial evidence so far, and Horace doesn't have a case. But the judge suggested Horace ride out with me and talk to you, Hildy. I've told him I'm satisfied you'll be honest with him."

"Shore she will!" Ruby blurted. She seemed to have gotten past any lingering anger she'd had with Hildy over their previous disagreement. "Hildy's as honest as the day is long. Tell 'em, Hildy!"

Hildy glanced at her stepmother, then Uncle Nate. When they both nodded encouragement, Hildy took a deep breath and started. "Mr. Taggett, I think you're letting your bigotry against what you call 'Okies' ruin my reputation. I had nothing to do with anything that isn't a hundred percent honest. I live my life as nearly as possible with a good conscience toward God and man. I wish you'd believe me."

The merchant raised a stubby finger as though he was going to point it at her. Instead, he lowered it to rest on his rumpled pant leg. "I don't think you did this alone, girlie," he said with controlled anger. "But I think somebody used you because you're a kid, and they didn't think I'd suspect you."

"Nobody used me!" Hildy exclaimed.

The merchant snapped, "Then why does everything in this mess revolve around you? Tell me that!"

With a patience she didn't feel, Hildy explained what she thought. It took some time to trace the events from her first seeing the watch through the various events culminating in returning the watch to the police.

"What I'd like you to do, Mr. Taggett," she concluded, "is work with Deputy Halden and the police chief. Maybe together we all can figure out how somebody learned about the map in the watch early Monday morning when I first came into your office.

"It's obvious that whoever that man was who first took the watch from you and knocked me down didn't know about the map until that morning. Otherwise, he'd have broken into your store between the time Alice Quayle pawned it Saturday night just before you closed and reopened Monday morning."

The deputy agreed. "That makes sense. Whoever robbed you, Horace, had to have found out about the watch Monday morning. Otherwise, Hildy's right. He'd have burglarized your place some time between Saturday night and early Monday morning."

"We've discussed everyone who might have known," the

pawnbroker said. "Alice didn't know, or she'd never have hocked the watch. So she's out. Her boyfriend didn't, or he would've kept her from pawning it. The lawyer certainly didn't. I've known him for years."

Taggett looked accusingly at Hildy. "So who else besides you knew about the watch?"

"Mr. Rawlins' law clerk and a couple of painters," Hildy replied. She still hurt from Merle Lamar's cruel remark when she first entered the attorney's office. But Hildy knew that didn't make him a criminal.

She had liked Peter Giles, the painter who had been nice to her when she staggered into the office where he was working on a ladder next door to the law office. She'd never seen the second painter, Dick Archer, so she didn't know anything about him.

The deputy consulted his notebook. "You've named six people who knew about the watch: Alice Quayle and her boyfriend, Bob Medwin; Merle Lamar, the law clerk; his employer, Attorney Seth Rawlins; and the painters, Giles and Archer. From a logical viewpoint, all of them can be freed of suspicion except the two painters. Right?"

Hildy hesitated, unwilling to let her personal antagonistic feelings about the law clerk become a factor in naming him. But she had no choice. "Don't forget Mr. Lamar," she said.

Taggett frowned as though unwilling to release his strong bias against Hildy. "And don't forget to include yourself," he said pointedly. "You claim you didn't know about the watch, but that's the only thing you asked to see when you entered my business that morning."

Hildy felt her emotions stir at the unjust suggestion. "I came in and looked around," Hildy corrected him. "I didn't see anything I liked until I saw that watch locked in the counter case. So I asked if I could see it."

She hesitated, then added, "If you're going to include everyone who knew about the watch, then your name has to be included, too."

"Me?" Taggett jumped up and stood on his short, stubby

legs. His face flushed red to his bald scalp. "If you're implying that I had anything to do with this—!"

"Easy, Horace!" the deputy said firmly, standing up quickly. He reached out to lay a restraining hand on the angry merchant's arm. "I think we've finished our business here. Let's get back to town."

Hildy said contritely, "Mr. Taggett, I didn't mean to upset—"

"Don't speak to me!" the merchant broke in. He rushed to the door and slid it open. He turned back to warn, "I'm not finished with you yet!" He pushed through the door and out of sight.

Hildy felt terrible, especially since she hadn't done anything wrong. She certainly didn't deserve such treatment or threats.

Deputy Halden seemed to sense her thoughts. He said, "Don't let his words hurt you, Hildy. I'll work on this case until it's solved."

She nodded her thanks and followed him to the door. He stopped suddenly. "Oh, I almost forgot! The sheriff got a call this morning from the sheriff in Miwuk County. He reported that the owner of Howling Cave said someone tried to break into his place last night."

"The cave? Odell Shanley's cave?"

The deputy nodded. "The person used a hacksaw to cut through two bars, but the third one was only partially sawed. Needed all three off to squeeze in. He probably got scared away, or daylight was coming or something so that he had to quit without gaining entry."

"You understand what that means, don't you?" Hildy asked.

"Yes, and so does the sheriff of Miwuk County. Whoever stole the map from the watch is trying to get to the treasure or whatever's indicated by the X on the map. But it won't do any good."

"How so?" Hildy asked.

"Because I understand Shanley's taken lights and explored everything around the X you told us you'd seen marked on the map. He didn't find anything. After all, it's been about seventy years. So even if the person breaks into the cave, he'll find that whatever he was after is long gone."

"Maybe Odell just overlooked it?" Hildy suggested.

"He doesn't think so," the deputy replied. He nodded to the others, then grinned at Hildy. "I'm on your side," he assured her. "I want to solve this case and help you clear your name. Well, see you later. And don't worry!"

But Hildy did worry. When the deputy had gone, Hildy turned to the others. "Maybe the reason Shanley couldn't find the exact spot is because he's never even seen the map with the X on it."

Ruby snorted. "If'n the crook cain't break in, then it don't matter none!"

Hildy started to nod in agreement, then stopped. "Mr. Shanley said there are some other entrances to the cave. When I looked at the map, I wondered if lines that looked like roads really were ways inside the cave—maybe like tunnels or passageways. Those lines must lead to the other cave entrances. I'd better tell—"

Hildy left her thought unfinished to race to the door. She slid it open, ready to call for the deputy to stop. But his car was already pulling onto the paved county road.

Hildy turned back into the room. "I guess it's all right. I don't need to tell the deputy, because Mr. Shanley knows about the other entrances. So he'll probably keep an eye on them, too. Besides, maybe whoever took the map won't realize what those lines are. Oh, if only there was some way I could get up there!"

Ruby shot a pleased look at her father, then spoke to Hildy. "Maybe yore 'bout to git yore wish, Hildy! Jist a-fore them men come by, him'n' me," she indicated her father with a nod, "was a-fixin' to drive up thar."

Hildy was vaguely uneasy that her cousin hadn't called her father "Daddy" or anything like that for some time. Ruby's use of 'him'n' me' suggested a continued downhill slide of their strained relationship.

"Now?" Hildy exclaimed. "How can you get off work, Uncle Nate?"

His face sobered. "Change o' plans. The church jist sent word that they got to move my preachin' date up."

"Move it up?" Hildy cried. "To when?"

"Tomorry." There was a sadness in her uncle's voice.

"Tomorrow?" Hildy glanced in disbelief at her uncle and cousin. "That can't be!"

"It's true, raht enough," Ruby said with a small smile. "'Leven o'clock tomorry mornin'. Reg'lar Sunday services, 'ceptin' he's a-gonna preachify!"

Hildy suddenly understood why Ruby had been so relaxed. Her father's fleece sermon had suddenly taken the worst possible turn against him. Hildy loved her cousin, but she was sick about what tomorrow could mean to her uncle.

Hildy caught at a straw. "You can't go tomorrow! You've got no car!"

Ruby cried, "Oh yes, he has! Man we work fer, Mr. Gilbert, done loaned us this ol' Model T. Reckon maybe it'll make it up them steep hills. If not—" She shrugged.

Hildy understood that Ruby meant it was too bad if her father's car broke down and he didn't even show up for the sermon. Did that also mean Ruby didn't care about possibly seeing Spud? Hildy wasn't sure. But she was sure of one thing: There was no logical way that the church would be full after the sudden change of dates.

Hildy felt sick at the thought of what the failure of this test fleece would do to her uncle. And what would it do to the already strained relationships between Ruby and her father?

Nate Konning announced, "We'uns have to go back to the Gilberts' to git muh suit an' Ruby's dress fer church. We come off sudden-like when them men showed up. You want to go with us, Hildy?"

Hildy pushed aside thoughts of an empty church. Her mind flashed to images of Spud, sick at Widow Benton's place. Hildy looked questioningly at her stepmother.

Molly seemed to read Hildy's anguished thoughts. "Go along, Hildy," she said. "Check on Spud, and see Mr. Shanley. I can handle the girls and the baby all right. But please take your pet. I'm sure Mrs. Benton will let you leave Mischief at her place during the church service."

Hildy raced to get her only Sunday dress and last year's good shoes. In a few minutes she had packed everything in an old cardboard suitcase and perched Mischief on her shoulder.

Hildy walked out of the house with mixed feelings of hope and despair at what she was going to see.

CHAPTER SEVENTEEN

STRANDED!

Within ten minutes Hildy realized that this trip was going to be hard. The sun's rays were intense, made worse by the dry, heated wind generated by the car's momentum. The searing wind blasted painfully across the girl's face.

"Sure a scorcher!" Hildy said, raising her voice to Ruby, who was on Hildy's right in the backseat of the topless old Model T. Mischief was on Hildy's left.

"Whut?" Ruby answered, leaning close to Hildy.

"It's sure hot!" Hildy yelled back.

Hildy wished she'd brought a hat to prevent sunburn. But the hot wind would have made it impossible to wear a light-weight feminine hat in the open car. However, her uncle, like her father, never ventured outdoors without a wide brimmed hat. Uncle Nate had pulled his sweat-stained tapered western hat down firmly on his forehead. It stayed in place.

Hildy was bursting with questions and thoughts. *Is Spud all right? Is he still at Mrs. Benton's? Wonder what Ruby's thinking?* Hildy thought of something else. She turned to her cousin and shouted, "You going to hold your father to that fleece test?"

Ruby leaned closer. "Why not?"

"It's not fair, that's why!" Hildy felt the hot summer breeze snatch her words away. Her throat already felt strained from the necessity of shouting.

"Deal's a deal!"

Hildy felt unaccustomed anger rise up in her mouth like the taste of brass. She wanted to shake some sense into her cousin. But Hildy knew it would take something else to make Ruby see what was about to happen.

Ruby wanted a father—but on her own terms. She didn't want one who preferred her in dresses rather than boys' clothes. Ruby certainly didn't want a preacher for her parent. Tomorrow, Ruby seemed certain to get what she wanted. If she cared about the cost of failure to her father, Ruby didn't show it. She seemed to look forward to the results as a personal triumph.

Hildy glanced at her uncle in the front seat. His eyes were fixed straight ahead toward the mountains. He kept trying to square his shoulders, but they tended to slip into a slight hunch. Hildy wondered if he was fighting discouragement.

Hildy closed her eyes. "Lord," she prayed silently, "I don't know what to do, but I want Ruby and her father to get along. At least let some people be there tomorrow to hear him preach. And, please help Spud to be all right so he can go on home to his parents before it's too late." She hesitated, wanting to ask that Spud still be at Mrs. Benton's, but decided not to pray for that.

Hildy opened her eyes, feeling more confident. That feeling was immediately challenged as the first foothills slowed the car's momentum. Hildy felt the Model T slacken its rattling pace. The really big hills were still ahead.

Hildy shook off sudden doubts that the ancient vehicle would complete the trip. She looked over to Mischief as the raccoon stirred. Hildy understood about the blistering heat on the old seat, especially where it had cracked. Coiled springs and stiff, black horsehair stuffing poked through. Hildy eased Mischief onto her lap and spoke reassuring words to her pet.

Thunder Mountain was still an hour's drive ahead when Hildy heard her uncle exclaim, "Oh no!"

Hildy glanced at him and then immediately beyond to the radiator. Steam was pouring out.

Hildy leaned forward, anxiously watching the rising clouds of steam. Ruby also leaned forward, but she didn't seem as concerned. That annoyed Hildy, but she kept silent as the sound of the boiling radiator and escaping steam got worse.

"No use!" Uncle Nate finally said. "Cain't go on without water. Yonder's some." He steered the Model T onto the shoulder.

No ranch house was visible on the lonely, deserted rolling hills that stretched to the horizon in every direction. However, a hundred feet inside the barbed wire fence on the right, a lone windmill pumped water into a concrete trough. White-faced Herefords watched the stranded motorists for a moment, then turned and thundered away together, tails high. Hildy wondered how they found nourishment in the dry grass.

"Lemme see if I kin find somethin' to tote water in," Uncle Nate said.

The girls got out of the backseat. Mischief complained with plaintive little cries as Hildy lifted the animal in her arms. The cousins stood in dry weeds beside the highway while Nate rummaged through the crippled vehicle for some kind of container.

Hildy glanced up and down the highway. No other cars were in sight. The road was silent except for the whispered passing of the hot, dry wind and a red-tailed hawk that screamed overhead.

Hildy's eyes lifted to the rolling hills on all sides. They were treeless and barren except for short yellow-brown grass. The searing wind wafted the pungent stench of tarweed into Hildy's nostrils.

Hildy dropped her gaze to the windmill, hoping for shade to protect Mischief. There was no tank house, just the metal frame holding up the tin sails and the trough.

Ruby asked, "Kinda lonesome-like, ain't it?"

Hildy didn't answer. She wondered if her cousin wanted them to fail in getting to Thunder Mountain. But if that happened, Ruby wouldn't get to see Spud—if he was still there.

Maybe, Hildy decided, *she doesn't care.*

Uncle Nate straightened up. "Cain't find nothin'! Reckon I'll hafta use muh hat." He glanced at the water trough. "But I'll hafta wait 'til the radiator cools off so's I kin touch it. Be half hour er so."

Hildy felt her pet. The fur was hot to the touch. "I've got to get Mischief into some shade. But if I put her in what little the car makes, she might run out in the road and get killed if another car goes by."

Her uncle said, "Only other shade they is is what ye'd git hunkered down by that trough. Be muddy, though."

"I'll try it," Hildy decided. She turned toward the fence with Mischief in her arms. "Coming, Ruby?" Hildy wanted to talk with her cousin without being overheard.

"Reckon so," Ruby answered.

Nate announced he'd stay by the Model T and try to flag down any motorist who passed.

Hildy cradled Mischief in her arms as Ruby put one foot on a lower strand of wire. She gingerly lifted the next one up so Hildy could ease through. Then Hildy repeated the action for Ruby. The cousins walked through the smelly tarweed to a dry spot by the overflowing water trough. They sat down in three feet of shade.

It wasn't at all comfortable, which added to Hildy's frustration and annoyance with her cousin. Hildy's seething thoughts made her speak up, but carefully. "How're you and your father getting along?"

"Tolerable well, I reckon. He's done quit tormentin' me ever' blesset minute 'bout muh hair an' clothes. 'Course, he ain't given up. He's jist not sayin' nothin', so neither'm I."

"Ruby, that's no way to live! It'll just get worse and worse! You'll be together in one way, living under the same roof, but miles apart in all the other important ways. Like loving and caring and respecting each—"

"Oh, hesh up! I done made up muh mind. Tomorry, after this test is over and he comes to his senses, things'll work out. Then we kin plan to go back to the Ozarks afore school starts here. I kin show him off and brag on him and make all them people eat crow that was so mean to me all them years."

She paused, breathing fast with excitement, anticipating what a triumph it would be. "Ye ort to come with us, Hildy. Maybe make up with yore granny."

Hildy had enough problems at hand that she didn't want to think about her grandmother, but she decided it was useless to say anything else to Ruby about tomorrow. Hildy let her thoughts slip toward Spud.

It was as though Ruby had exactly the same idea. She adjusted her back to a more comfortable position against the trough. "What'd ye reckon happened to Spud? What kinda sickness did he git?"

"I don't know. I just hope he's all right."

"Me too." Ruby's words were almost a whisper.

Hildy glanced sharply at her cousin, not quite sure the plaintive two words had really been spoken. Ruby slapped at her overalls. "Wisht I'd a-wore me a dress!"

Hildy's lips twitched as she thought, *For Spud, but not your father!* The thought bothered Hildy so much that she abruptly changed the subject. "Ruby, if you hold your father to that fleece test tomorrow, you'll both be sorry!"

"Maybe *he* will, but *I* won't. I'm raht glad the way it's turnin' out. I mean, if'n we even git thar a-tall."

Hildy had to bite her tongue to keep from answering sharply. Then she realized that Ruby also wanted to get there, but for another reason. Hildy had two reasons; Ruby had only one.

Hildy forced her voice to sound calm. "We'll get there somehow. But don't you know what it might do to your father if nobody shows up tomorrow?"

"Shore do! He'll hafta quit raggin' me 'bout wearin' dresses and lettin' muh hair grow long an' actin' like a lady an' goin' to church reg'lar, an' all sech things."

Hildy's tone grew sharp with disapproval. "Did it ever occur to you that Uncle Nate might go back to his old ways if he's a big failure in his first attempt to live the way he feels God wants him to do?"

"Ain't likely. He ain't had nary a drink o' likker since he got saved. Ain't cussed ner nothin'. If'n he jist wouldn't keep a-talkin' about bein' called to preach, and tryin' to change me—well, he'd be a mighty tolerable daddy."

Hildy saw that as a small glimmer of hope for her cousin and uncle. "He said he was once like Jonah, running away from God. What if nobody shows up tomorrow, and he's so hurt that he runs again?"

"He wouldn't do no sich a thing! We found each other, and we air a-gonna stay together!"

Hildy didn't try to reason anymore. She glanced around at their merciless surroundings.

All the winter and spring snowpack from the high Sierras had long ago melted and flowed down canals into the valley for irrigation use. In the distance, Hildy could see a small ravine. She knew it would have a dry, cracked bottom. The ravine wouldn't be entirely lifeless. The sides would be occupied by tiny billy owls, small cottontails and perhaps a diamondback rattlesnake.

It was a lonely and dreary place. Not a single car had come along the highway from either direction since the Ford had broken down. In the fifth year of the Depression, people traveled only when necessary. The whole setting tended to make Hildy discouraged.

She glanced up as her uncle rose from the shade cast by the Model T. He raised his voice to the girls. "Reckon it's cooled off enough by now."

Hildy watched as he walked to the radiator and examined it. He shook his head and called, "It done more than b'ile dry. It's broke."

Hildy pushed herself up from the water trough's shade, anxiety clawing at her insides. "You mean we're stuck here?"

Ruby said softly, "Shore sounds that way."

Uncle Nate shifted the hat to a new position on his head, then stiffened. "Car comin'!" he called. "Slowin' up, I think."

Hildy turned to look back down toward the valley. A lone vehicle was rounding a curve. She blinked and stared. "That's a yellow Packard. Say, that looks like—it is! That's Brother Ben!"

The girls and raccoon had barely crawled through the barbed wire fence to the roadway when the old ranger stopped. He stepped off the running board to the roadway and gave his yellowish-white handlebar mustache a flip. "You folks burned to a crisp?"

Hildy ran toward the tall, stately old gentleman. The raccoon in her arms complained about the jostling with sharp little sounds.

Ruby outran Hildy and reached Brother Ben first. "Howdy!" she cried. "We been broke down fer the longest time. Kin ye give us a lift home?"

Ben raised the white cowboy hat and wiped his brow with a clean white handkerchief. "I'd like to, Ruby, but I'm on my way up to Thunder Mountain. Be glad to give all of you a ride there if you'd like."

Hildy thought she saw just a touch of smile on Brother Ben's lips. Hildy glanced at her cousin and saw disappointment. Hildy didn't care. She felt very good at the change in circumstances.

In moments they had transferred Hildy's cardboard suitcase and the Konnings' cracked wicker one to the Packard. All three stranded motorists slid into the yellow car's shaded interior. Brother Ben eased out onto the highway, leaving the Model T behind.

As they started up the winding road, the old ranger looked in his rearview mirror at the girls in the backseat. He said, "Hildy, I stopped by your place a while ago. Molly told me what had happened and where you folks were headed. I'm sorry about Spud. Hope he's all right."

He shifted his gaze to the man sitting beside him. "Nate, I didn't want to miss hearing your first sermon, either. So I headed this way fast's I could go. Looks like it was a good thing too."

Hildy dropped her head so Ruby couldn't see the smile that formed on her lips.

It was getting on toward dusk when the Packard turned off onto the treeless driveway leading straight to the foot of Thunder Mountain. The dugout showed ahead.

Ruby announced, "Somebody's a-raisin' the door. It's Jacob an' his sisters."

The Benton children erupted from the sod house. They dashed forward, recognizing the familiar yellow Packard.

Hildy was glad to see them, but she was more anxious to know if Spud had recovered from his illness. Was he still here?

Another face showed at the dugout door, and Mrs. Benton stepped out onto the bare ground. She called a warning to the children. They scattered obediently to one side to avoid danger from the approaching vehicle.

Hildy's anxious eyes flickered back to the dugout door. It was closed.

Hildy sighed, thinking, *Spud's not here. Guess he's gone on toward New York. Or—"*

A terrible possibility struck her. Maybe he got worse and—!

She tried to shake off the awful thought, but it scared her as the Packard stopped and the Benton kids raced toward it.

"Are they bringing bad news?" Hildy asked herself. She swallowed hard, awaiting the answer.

CHAPTER EIGHTEEN

THE CHURCH AT THUNDER MOUNTAIN

Jacob and the two sisters just younger than he jumped up on both running boards and stuck their heads inside the Packard. They reached eager hands in to welcome their guests, especially Mischief. The dugout was a lonely spot in a lonely land without neighbors, radio, telephone, or newspapers. Company was rare.

"Howdy, ever'body!" Ten-year-old Jacob cried. "Light an' sit a spell." His invitation came with a wide grin.

Hildy sighed with relief, recognizing that their actions meant Spud was either all right or had gone on toward New York. Still, Hildy wanted to ask about Spud, but seven-year-old Rachel and four-year-old Becky were jabbering away with excitement. Their hair was neatly combed. Their dresses were thin with age, but clean, neat, and patched.

Their widowed mother reached the car, carrying Becky, who was nearly two. She in turn carried her ever-present, empty Cola-Cola bottle by the baby's nipple on top. Mrs. Benton shushed her excited children, waving them back so the visitors could alight from the Packard.

The widow's hair was neatly combed and done up in a bun. Her dress was old but freshly washed. Her rimless glasses perched far down on her nose. She looked quite nice, Hildy thought.

"We bin expectin' y'all," Mrs. Benton said with a smile. She bobbed her head in greeting to everyone, but Hildy noticed the widow seemed to look at Uncle Nate a tiny bit longer, and her smiled widened a little more.

Hildy also noticed that Ruby's father seemed to return the smile with a trifle more pleasure than he gave the four Benton children. Hildy shot a glance at her cousin, but Ruby apparently hadn't notice anything.

As everyone got out of the car, Hildy shot another look toward the dugout. She reluctantly concluded that Spud wasn't in there, or he'd have come out by now.

She wanted to ask, just to be sure, but there was still too much commotion from the eager Benton children. Hildy decided they probably inherited that tendency from their mother. The first time Hildy had met Mrs. Benton, words had poured out of the woman in an endless stream. She was still gushing.

"Hildy, if'n ye don't mind, let my young'uns pet yore coon. They'll be plumb keerful. I declare! They hardly done nothin' but talk 'bout that thar little critter since you'ns left!"

Hildy held Mischief out to eager hands. "Jacob, you get to hold her first because you're the oldest. Then take turns. If you quarrel, nobody gets to hold her."

The children agreed, as their mother led the way toward the dugout.

"We done set extry plates an' held up supper," she explained. "An' we got 'nough blankets an' quilts an' sech like so's ever'-body kin sleep comfor'able, too. Want ever'body to be well fed and slept out afore your sermon tomorry, Mr. Konning."

"I'm obliged, Mrs. Benton," he said, smiling down from his great height at her. "An' please call me Nate."

"Well, if'n yore shore. All right—Nate. Only it don't hardly seem fittin' to call a preacher by—"

"He ain't no preacher!" Ruby's interruption was so sharp and unexpected that it stopped all conversation cold. Even the children's incessant chatter was stilled.

Brother Ben jumped in quickly, breaking the embarrassing silence with his soft, easy drawl. "Missus Benton, you look mighty perky."

Nate added, "I was jist a-thinkin' the same thing."

"Thankee both," she replied, smiling at the men. "But please call me Rebekah. Jist like in the Bible."

Ruby's outburst seemed forgotten as they neared the dugout. Hildy looked ahead, still vainly hoping to see Spud. Out of the corner of her eye, Hildy saw that Ruby was also stealing glances at the sod house.

Hildy couldn't stand the suspense any longer. "Mrs. Benton, where's Spud?"

"Why, didn't we tell y'all? I declare! We'uns all been a-talkin' so hard it plumb slipped my mind! He'll be back direc'ly, Hildy. He an' my young'uns made a bunch of flyers tellin' about the change in service to tomorry. I guess they handed them out to about ever' shack and house in these parts."

Hildy had trouble letting out a long, slow sigh of relief so it wasn't noticeable.

Jacob pointed. "Yonder he comes!"

Hildy spun around, her long braids flying out so fast and hard they struck her cousin. Ruby had also whirled around. The girls stood side by side in the dust.

Spud jogged ahead of Lindy. As Spud waved, his dog gave a single joyous yelp and broke into a hard run. Seconds later, the Airedale was thrusting his broad head alternately under Hildy's and Ruby's caressing hands.

Spud stopped with a grin before the cousins. Hildy thought the freckles on his face and hands seemed to stand out sharply because his ruddy complexion had faded.

"Greetings and felicitations!" he cried, his green eyes as bright as his smile. Then he glanced at Ruby and challenged her. "You going to make your usual pejorative remarks to me?"

Hildy expected Ruby's typical cutting remarks about Spud's tendency to use big words. That always resulted in another argument between them.

Instead, Ruby smiled. "I reckon I'm a-gittin' used to yore big words," she said softly. She added, "I kinda like 'em nowadays."

Hildy felt her insides leap and twist, but she wasn't quite sure why.

Everyone, including the dog and raccoon, took the few stairs from the cellar-like door to the dugout. The fragrance of hot bread and boiling potatoes came from the wood-burning cookstove below.

"Mrs. Benton, ye got a place I kin change clothes?" Ruby asked. "I brought me a dress to wear."

"I'll be double-whupped fer a hoss thief!" Ruby's father muttered in total surprise.

Ruby said a little defensively, "These ol' clothes got fulla grit an' sand on the ride up."

Mrs. Benton pointed. "Me'n the kids strung a clothesline acrost the back end o' the room so's we kin have privacy fer sleepin'. Ye kin change thar."

Hildy glanced around the single large room. It was below ground except for about three feet closest to the nearly flat roof. Made entirely of sun-dried adobe brick, the room was remarkably cool. Small windows under the roof stood open for the cool evening breeze that had just sprung up. Broom marks were clearly visible where the dirt floor had been thoroughly swept.

Ruby changed behind the makeshift screen made by quilts, tablecloths, and old sheets draped over the clothesline and clipped in place with clothespins.

Everyone else sat on boards laid across lug boxes to create benches. A table had been made with lugs set on end and placed before the benches.

Hildy looked across at Spud. "Thanks for your letter. You all right now?"

"I'm fine," he assured her.

"What happened?"

"I apparently picked up some malevolent germs. I could feel

a fever starting while I was riding with a truck driver shortly after we left Lone River. I was sick as a dog when we got near Thunder Mountain. I didn't know if I was going to die or not, but I certainly didn't want to die by the roadside. I told the truck driver about this place, and he brought me here."

"Yeah!" Jacob added, running up, carrying Mischief. "He was sicker'n a hoss! Ma like to a-wore me out runnin' to the crick to fetch cold water. She soaked rags an' put 'em on his head."

Mrs. Benton explained, "They wasn't nothin' else a body could do. No medicines er money fer doctors. Jist the cool rags. Well, I reckon some powerful prayin' he'ped. The fever finally broke. Last couple days he's been fit as a fiddle string."

Hildy didn't want to ask, but she had to know. "When're you going to continue toward your parents?"

"Monday. I felt well enough to start sooner, but I wanted to hear the Shepherd of Thunder Mountain give his first sermon."

Hildy was surprised. "You're going to hear him?"

"Wouldn't miss it."

Ruby came out from behind the screen straightening her dress. She muttered, "Ever'body else will. Reckon they won't be a dozen people show up."

Hildy wanted to cry, *You'd like that, wouldn't you? You'd like it even though that'd hurt your father far worse than you can imagine!* Instead, she held her tongue, berating herself for her own feelings toward Ruby.

What's the matter with me? she asked herself sternly. *Ruby's my best friend! She's a good person, too! Got to get hold of myself.*

Still, there was a tenseness inside Hildy that wouldn't go away the rest of the evening.

Supper was served. With some gentle, good-natured shifting and holding elbows tight to their bodies, everyone was seated. The hostess asked Nate to return thanks. It was the last quiet moment, because throughout the simple meal conversations erupted and flowed endlessly.

When it was over, Ruby surprised Hildy by insisting on washing the dishes. Hildy dried, alternating her thoughtful gaze between her cousin and everybody else. Especially Spud.

Uncle Nate asked to be excused. He went outside alone. Hildy guessed it was to pray and review his sermon notes. Ruby and Spud talked without arguing. Mischief seemed to sense Hildy's internal discomfort. The little coon crawled up in her lap and nuzzled her chin like a kitten.

Hildy was glad when the little children went to sleep. Two hours later everyone else was asleep—except her. She lay awake, staring unseeingly at the darkened ceiling, barely aware of the snoring from various temporary compartments of cloth and clothesline.

I'm sorry to feel the way I do toward Ruby, Hildy told herself. *But it's her fault that tomorrow Uncle Nate has to lay a fleece before the Lord. The next day, Spud leaves for the East. Will I ever see him again?*

Her thoughts surged and changed. *When I get home, there's all the trouble with Mr. Taggett. Until whoever stole that watch and later took the map is caught and confesses, my name's not going to be cleared.*

She rolled that idea around in her mind. *That robber's got to be caught! But how can he when nobody knows who he is?*

Her lips moved silently. "Lord, I'm sick of all the terrible things coming up! Please help me through them."

The morning started out orderly enough. Breakfast consisted of fresh biscuits, hot oatmeal mush, fried leftover potatoes and brown gravy.

Brother Ben had brought milk kept on ice in a bucket in the Packard's trunk. For the first time, Mrs. Benton said, all the children had milk for breakfast. Usually, she only had canned condensed milk for the baby's bottle.

The pace increased as everyone tried to get ready for church. There was no bathroom and no running water, and only one white granite pan for bathing. Buckets of water from the creek were poured in the pan, which was then emptied and refilled as one person after another stepped behind a curtain for what Mrs. Benton called a "spit bath" that included rags for wash-cloths.

There weren't any towels, so each bather's body had to dry

in the air before clothes could be put on. The Benton family donned shoes that didn't really fit any of them. Hildy recognized the shoes as those that had been brought up in boxes of used clothing donated by her church in Lone River.

At last, clean but a little tense from all the hurrying, everyone was ready. Mischief and Lindy were left in the cool dugout. Brother Ben slid behind the wheel of the Packard with Nate Konning beside him. Mrs. Benton held the baby in the right-front passenger's seat.

Jacob sat on Spud's lap in the right corner of the backseat. Ruby, in her dress and perky little hat, had squeezed in next to him.

Ruby said, "Rhonda, ye kin sit on muh lap 'cause yore littler an' won't wrinkle muh dress."

Hildy held seven-year-old Rachel, unmindful of her dress. Hildy had much more important things on her mind than wrinkled clothes.

There was a tension in the car during the drive along the country road paralleling Thunder Mountain. Even the children were silent, sensing something important was about to happen.

Hildy was becoming uncomfortable from holding the little girl in such cramped quarters when the Packard slowed. Hildy could see the tall steel structures supporting high-voltage wires, and soon the driver made the right turn leading to the church at Thunder Mountain.

Hildy wondered why the congregation had been so divided that few people now attended and no pastor would stay. She did know that her uncle would be preaching his first sermon under the worst circumstances imaginable.

Hildy closed her eyes briefly. She wanted to pray, but no words came, not even thoughts she could organize. Instead, she felt a heaviness that made her moan silently.

Hildy opened her eyes, sensing everyone in the packed car was starting to lean forward, straining to see ahead. The Packard topped a small brown hill. As the vehicle started down, the first sign of a building gradually appeared on the horizon.

The white wooden cross atop the church steeple showed first

like a small, white beacon of hope in a barren and desolate land.

Hildy's eyes dropped lower. In one of the few acre flats commonly tucked into the rolling foothills, the simple white frame building gradually appeared from the top down. As the Packard approached, the church glistened silently in the morning sun.

Everything else was as Hildy remembered it. The small white porch in front. Lean-to in back. Two outhouses at the far end. The unkempt cemetery. The wide graveled church yard with hitching rails.

Wait! Hildy's thoughts snapped her eyes into a sharp focus. *Everything's not the same as before!* Hildy leaned forward so hard and suddenly that Rachel let out an involuntary grunt.

The churchyard, so lonely and silent when Hildy had seen it before, had come alive. Horses with buggies twitched their tails and munched feed bags at the hitching rails. There were also roadsters, touring cars, coupes, and a few closed sedans parked away from the horses.

Most dramatic of all, the yard in front of the church was alive with men, women, and children!

Brother Ben steered his big car steadily along the country road to where it intersected with another. There vehicles were pulling off onto the wide shoulders. Automobiles that had arrived earlier were already parked all around the church.

"Golly!" Jacob breathed the word in awe. "Fur's a body kin see they's cars! An' people!"

Hildy nodded in silent wonder. Men and women of all ages, accompanied by children, flowed toward the small white symbol of hope, where a former drunken sheepherder was to deliver his first sermon.

Hildy got out of the car feeling hot tears start behind her eyeballs and ooze out the far corners of her eyes. Then the tears slid unnoticed down her cheeks.

For a moment, everyone from the Packard stood in silence, looking at the unbelievable. Then Jacob whispered in awe, "Must be a hunnert people!"

"Maybe not that many," Nate Konning replied in a hushed voice. "But enough to show that the Lord has prepared the way."

Someone on the front porch reached up and pulled a long rope dangling about six feet from the floor. The bell in the steeple pealed loudly, clearly. Then, as it gathered momentum, it rang out again and again, sending a message of invitation and welcome on the morning air.

As the clarion call echoed off Thunder Mountain, Nate Konning squared his shoulders. "Come on, everybody," he said quietly.

"Yeah!" Jacob added, "We gotta hurry before they's not a seat left fer us!"

CHAPTER
NINETEEN

A MORNING OF DECISION

As they entered the church, Spud whispered to Hildy, "It's sparse but functional."

Her eyes followed his. There were three six-foot-high oblong windows on each side of the small white-frame sanctuary. The windows were open to let any stray breeze waft across the worshipers. A hand-carved redwood cross hung behind the homemade pulpit. It was flanked by two straight-backed chairs. Two rows of ancient wooden pews were separated by an aisle in the middle. A small curved altar rested on the wooden floor between the front row of pews and the raised pulpit platform.

Hildy felt grateful that there were so many people in attendance. Then she became tense and concerned over how well Uncle Nate would do before such a crowd. Would he get nervous and not do well? *Well,* she thought with satisfaction, *at least he's met Ruby's fleece.* Then Hildy corrected herself. *I mean, the Lord has.*

Hildy tried to see how her cousin was taking this, but Ruby kept her face turned away as everyone from the Packard took seats down front on the left side of the aisle.

Brother Ben sat on the far end nearest the side door. Mrs. Benton and her four children were next. Jacob was beside Hildy on her left. Spud sat between Hildy and Ruby. Uncle Nate sat stiffly in the left-hand straight-backed chair beside the pulpit. He looked very uncomfortable in a blue serge suit and brown shoes.

A portly old cattleman perspired in a too-tight gray suit beside the guest preacher. A young cowboy in mismatched coat and pants stood up to announce that "Onward, Christian Soldiers" would be the first hymn. An older woman with her gray hair parted in the middle and drawn back severely in a tight bun began playing the introduction on an out-of-tune upright piano.

During the singing of the first verse, Hildy twisted her head to look around. She quickly counted six rows of plain wooden pews with six persons on each side of the center aisle. Some folding chairs had been placed in back by the double doors. The two ushers were standing.

Hildy was overjoyed at the remarkable attendance. She turned around and whispered to Spud, "Place is packed to the rafters! Must be seventy-five people!"

"Eighty-one," Spud whispered back.

Hildy bent forward to look beyond Spud to Ruby, who was not singing. She held a broken-backed red hymnal, but her mouth was shut in a tight thin line.

She's mad! Hildy thought. *She didn't want anybody to show up. But her fleece test is sure confirmed.*

For a moment that gave Hildy a sense of pleasure. Then she silently reprimanded herself. *I'm glad for Uncle Nate, but Ruby must hurt terribly inside!*

Hildy's reflections were interrupted as her uncle rose unexpectedly from his chair. He stepped up beside the young song leader. "'Scuse me, brother," Nate said.

Hildy was startled as the congregational song broke off into ragged remnants. The piano player paused, her fingers suspended above the yellowed keys. Nobody was more surprised than the song leader. His eyes widened as the guest preacher turned to the congregation.

"Y'all please fergive me fer a-bustin' up yore singin' like this. I'm jist a man, ordinary as a dirt clod, 'cept fer one thing: I got somethin' to sing about. I been a-wantin' to jine y'all in singin' a good ol' gospel song so's it'd lift my socks raht outta muh shoes. No offense, folks, but we'uns is a-draggin' this here song plumb to death."

Hildy stared in disbelief as her uncle turned to the piano player. "Ma'am, yore a right good pie-anner player, an' I 'preciate whut yore a-doin'. Howsomever, I'd be obliged if'n ye let yorself go. Bang them keys faster!"

His hands swooped out in a wide gesture. "Fergit that some o' them keys stick, er sound wrong. Lemme hear ye make a joyful noise with that thar instr'ment. Like this." He started swinging his right hand vigorously in a double time.

The woman's fingers dropped to the keys, her eyes following Nate's enthusiastic but ungainly arm movements.

"That's it! That's it!" Nate cried approvingly as she struck the piano, producing an upbeat march tempo. He turned back to smile encouragingly at the song leader. "Now, brother, let's start over."

Nate turned back to the audience, his smile widening. "Ever'body let yoreselves go! Lemme see them rafters ring with joy!"

Hildy twisted anxiously as the piano set a pace that suggested feet marching triumphantly. The congregation caught the spirit and sang lustily, heads back, mouths wide.

Hildy glanced up at her uncle. He still stood behind the song leader, whose arms were now moving in quick, sharp strokes. Both he and the visiting preacher were singing with great gusto.

Spud stopped singing long enough to whisper to Hildy, "He's off to a mighty good start!"

When Nate stood from his chair to preach, Hildy sensed something almost electric in the packed church. He walked purposefully to the pulpit. He prayed aloud briefly, opened his Bible, and laid it across his open left palm. He raised his eyes to the congregation, but did not speak.

He's scared! Hildy thought in sudden alarm. *Looking out at all those faces made him forget whatever he was going to say. Oh, poor*

Uncle Nate! She groaned inwardly, then stopped and looked closer.

For a full thirty seconds, Nate Konning's eyes roamed the congregation. But Hildy suddenly realized he wasn't afraid. He was doing this deliberately, although she didn't know why. His gaze stopped momentarily—here, there, up front, in back. Nate seemed to look at every individual personally. He was doing more than meeting every eye; he was looking deeper, inside.

The silence built. There was no coughing, no nervous clearing of throats, no children fussing. There was absolute and total attention on the tall man in the pulpit.

Hildy was aware that she was holding her breath. She had no idea what her uncle's sermon topic was, no idea of his text or what he planned to say. He had kept that to himself.

Finally he spoke. His voice was low but clearly audible. "This here's cattle country. Yore cattlemen and cattlemen's families. Me? I used to be a cowboy, but now I'm jist a plain ol' sheepherder."

He stopped as though to let those contrasting thoughts sink in. Then he added, "But I'm in good company 'cause David was a shepherd. Jesus is our shepherd. So I'd be obliged if y'all'd put aside yore personal feelin's about sheepherders an' lemme tell ye a true story."

Hildy swallowed hard, sensing the emotion behind her uncle's words.

He paused again, eyes probing, seeking, then moving on before speaking again. "I reckon I'll make some of ye mad—maybe all of ye—afore I'm done."

A murmur rippled through the crowd, but Nate Konning's eyes never wavered. When the silence had again settled, he continued. "But when I'm done, they'll be somethin' said that'll he'p ever' single one of ye a-sittin' out thar today. Ye want the good. Ye got to hear the bad, too."

Hildy stole a glance at Ruby. Her mouth was relaxed slightly. The grim tightness was gone. Like the others, she was listening, although Hildy sensed her cousin and all others were waiting to see what would anger them.

Nate held up his Bible where it rested on his open left palm. He said, "So fur's I kin tell, Jesus only give one sign by which people could reco'nize His disciples. Ye'll find it in the thirteenth chapter of John and the thirty-fifth verse."

He waited while those who had brought Bibles riffled through the pages. Hildy wished she'd remembered to bring hers, because she didn't know that text.

When the pages stopped turning, the visiting preacher put his finger on the open Bible. "Accordin' to our Lord—an' I'm a-readin' His very words—'by this shall all men know that ye are my disciples, if ye have love one to another.' "

Nate closed the Bible with a snap and laid it on the pulpit. He stepped to the side so there was no physical barrier of any type between him and his listeners.

"Folks," Nate said so softly his voice could barely be heard, "it's come to my attention that some people hereabouts would have a hard time bein' reco'nized as the Lord's disciples, maybe even by the Lord hisself."

The blunt words brought an audible gasp. It seemed as if it came only from one person, yet the sound was so loud it had to come from many throats. Hildy was aware she had contributed to that reaction.

Spud leaned over and whispered hoarsely, "Talk about taking the bull by the horns! I hope he can make his point without being run out of town on a rail!"

Hildy felt her mouth go dry with fear for her uncle as he began building his sermon. "To love is to obey. Obedience is a choice. So's disobedience, but a wrong one."

Hildy heard a restless stirring in the congregation behind her. She wondered if Nate would be able to keep the congregation from walking out before he came to the personal benefits he'd promised before he was through.

"Now that I plumb got yore undivided attention," he said with a gentle smile, "lemme tell ye 'bout how a cowboy got to be a sheepherder."

The restless tension in the audience eased as the visiting preacher gave his brief testimony. He told about a wild, misspent youth, about meeting and marrying a young woman at a Texas camp meeting, of committing his life to God, then being disobedient to a call to preach. He briefly recounted his recent recommitment at a brush-arbor service. Then he returned to his story.

Nate never raised his voice as he told about his wife leaving him as he started drinking and drifting. He recalled his slide from respected cowboy to despised sheepherder, ending up here on Thunder Mountain. Finally, he told about recently learning his late wife had given birth to a daughter.

"'Til jist a couple weeks ago," he said in a hushed voice, "I didn't even know I had me a dotter. I'd admire fer all o' ye to know her."

Nate's eyes softened as he looked down at the front row. "No daddy ever had a finer dotter'n mine. She spent her life a-wantin' to find her daddy, an' she done it this very month."

Hildy stole a glance at Ruby, but she was leaning back so Spud blocked Hildy's view.

Uncle Nate continued. "Ye know why she kept a-lookin' 'til she found me? She had a hunger, a love hunger, fer a man she didn't even rahtly know was alive or dead. That love inside never let her give up. That love brought me an' her together, an' that love'll see us through ary other problems that kin come along in life."

Nate's voice cracked, drawing Hildy's eyes back to him. He continued. "Yonder sits muh dotter Ruby. She's comin' on to bein' a young woman, an' she's a-changin'. She's got a powerful mind o' her own, an' I respect that. But her heart's full o' love, jist like mine is, and that's whut's goin' to see us through our lives now that we air together fer the fust time."

He paused and held Ruby's eyes with his own, which clearly glistened brightly with tears. "Ruby, honey, I love ye with all muh heart. 'Cause I do, I done whut ye asked, and left the results in the Lord's hands."

He stopped, letting the reference to the fleece become clear in his daughter's mind. Hildy leaned forward slightly to look at her cousin, trying to understand what she was thinking. But

Ruby's face showed no visible emotion.

"Now," the preacher continued, again letting his probing eyes sweep the congregation, "let's talk a bit 'bout y'all."

Hildy didn't know where he had learned the history of the splintered church, but he obviously knew it well. Without any hint of names or blame, Nate Konning pointed out that the congregation was divided because they were guilty of not loving one another.

"Don't make no diff'runce if'n ye was plumb positive ye was raht and t'others daid wrong. Y'all done lost yore brand—the Lord's only sign that others could reco'nize ye was His'n. Y'all was disobedient to the Lord, an' that's yore choice, an' now yore a-payin' a turrible price."

Nate paused, silently letting his remarks sink in. Hildy wondered how others were taking it, but she didn't want to look around. Her uncle's words seemed to echo in her mind. It wasn't a matter of who was right and who was wrong, because everyone who hadn't loved was not obeying. The mark of discipleship was unconditional: love one another.

Nate started in again, gently chiding, softly urging, gradually building toward a climax.

"Look aroun' ye," Nate concluded softly. "See them good folks a-settin' thar? They air yore brothers an' sisters ever' blessit one of 'em!"

He had not raised his voice during the entire service, but now it rose to a thundering crescendo.

"An' while yore a-lookin' aroun', look inside and see if'n yore a reco'nizable disciple. An' if'n ye ain't—judgin' only by our Lord's sign—get up this blessit minute an' go make up with yore brother, yore sister! Say yore sorry! Make up with 'em! Then come down here to this hyar altar and make it raht with our Lord."

Nate's voice fell silent. He stood unmoving, except for his eyes. They probed again—here, there, everywhere. Hildy had a feeling he was looking inside every person, seeing the secrets there.

A strange silence settled over the mute crowd. Hildy was

scared to look around. She was fearful the whole packed house would rise as one and storm out in disapproval of the former sheepherder's blunt words.

Instead, a slow stirring sound began, softly at first, barely audible. Hildy stole cautious glances around. She saw individuals look hesitantly across the aisles to right and left and to those nearby. The stirring became a restless surge as individuals remembered and decided.

One stout matron jumped up with an anguished cry. She fairly threw herself across the aisle to sink, sobbing, before another woman.

It was like the first kernel of popcorn exploding in a hot pan. Faster and faster others also moved. They stood and walked resolutely to pews in front or back, across the aisles or wherever someone was who had been hurt or wronged, someone who had not been treated with love.

The movement grew, faster and faster, as people pushed their way to others with whom they obviously had disagreed. Soon it seemed as if the entire congregation was hugging and thumping one another on the back and weeping, asking forgiveness and granting it freely.

Hildy thought of her own unusual behavior and feelings toward her cousin. She leaned in front of Spud and touched Ruby's near arm. "I . . . I . . ." Hildy began, but her voice quivered and tears leaped unbidden to her eyes.

"It's aw'raht, Hildy," Ruby said, her eyes also bright; "we'uns got to talk, but fust I got to go hug muh daddy!"

Ruby fairly leaped from the front row and ran to the raised platform. Her father jumped down, his arms swinging wide to close about his daughter's body.

It was too personal and private a moment for Hildy. She looked away as a tear began sliding down her right cheek. Her vision was blurred, but she felt a gentle hand reach out and wipe the tear away. She turned to see Spud's eyes also were bright.

"Thanks," she said, sniffling and smiling at him.

He nodded but did not speak. Instead, he lowered his eyes

and looked at his big hands. Hildy also dropped her eyes, feeling such emotion that she could do nothing else.

Later, Nate Konning stood on the small church porch. He shook hands with the people patiently lined up—still choked with emotion—to say something to him. Ruby stood beside him, her nose red, her hat knocked sideways on her head, that important attire now forgotten.

Hildy felt a light touch on her elbow. She turned, thinking it was Brother Ben or Spud. Instead, she recognized Odell Shanley, owner of Howling Cave.

"Hello, Hildy," he said solemnly, his wild beard bobbing. "I thought you might be here. Everyone else is."

He turned and motioned for her to follow. "Please come outside, Hildy. I must talk to you right now."

She was too surprised to ask why. She followed the little man away from the clusters of people who had already spilled out into the churchyard. Near a Model A coupe with a rumble seat, Odell Shanley turned to face the girl. He lowered his voice. "Somebody broke into my cave last night."

"You mean he got inside?"

"Yes. You know, he failed to break in once before, but this morning I found where he'd broken in at one of the back entrances. That caused a rock slide, so he can't get out that way. Even if he could find the other two exits, he couldn't get out at either. Both have strong iron bars. So he's got to be inside somewhere."

Hildy was suddenly alarmed. "Why're you telling me?"

"You're the only one I know who has any idea where he must have been heading. That's wherever the gold—or whatever—is hidden. Hildy, I want you to help me find him."

"Go in that cave? No, Mr. Shanley. I can't! I'm terrified of such places!"

"Even if you know that man'll die if you don't?"

"What?"

"The engineers at the dam started filling one part today! That'll make the underground rivers in the cave start backing up as they do in winter. It'll fill the cave by nightfall."

While Hildy stared, fearful of what Odell meant, he concluded solemnly, "He'll try to go back out the way he came, and when he can't, he'll likely get lost. Then his light'll burn out and he'll drown in the dark!"

Hildy's insides churned suddenly and violently. She cried, "That's not my fault! He—whoever he is—has messed up my life! He's given me nothing but trouble! He's ruined my name! Why should I help him?"

"Because you're the only person who can. Now, what do you say, Hildy?"

CHAPTER
TWENTY
—

RACE FOR THE CAVE'S SECRET

A couple of hours later, Hildy stood with Spud and Ruby at the main entrance to Howling Cave. They had volunteered to go in with her and Odell. Brother Ben and Nate Konning had also offered, but the cave owner said he could move faster with the younger people. The adults had opposed the idea, but yielded to Odell because time was running out for the unknown man in the cave. So Ben and Nate, aided by little Jacob, were helping Odell prepare for the others to enter the caverns.

Hildy said in a small, scared voice, "I'll die if I go in there! I'm so scared of small, tight places!"

Spud nodded, looking at the iron bars over the cave's entrance. "Claustrophobia's a terrible thing, Hildy, but there's still time to back out. When Odell comes back, tell him you've changed your mind."

"But he said that person'll die in there if I don't go! If the rising underground river doesn't drown him, he'll run out of light. He'll get lost in the dark."

"Yore not the only one who seen the map he stole!" Ruby

protested. "I seen it; yore folks an' sisters, too. I'd go by myself, without ye, but I don't remember that map as good as ye do."

"I couldn't ask you, or any of them, to do what I won't do myself. Besides, we're racing the clock, because Odell says that underground river'll rise fast!"

Hildy shuddered, thinking of how awful it would be to die alone, without light or food, in the total blackness of a cave four hundred feet underground.

Holding Mischief in her left arm, Hildy stood in an old dress and her Sunday shoes, because Odell had recommended them over bare feet.

Ruby had put on a boy's jeans, shirt and shoes.

Spud wore his cowboy outfit. He said, "Here they come with the lights, ropes and things. Hildy, this's your last chance to change your mind. Remember, you don't owe that crook anything!"

Hildy shook her head. "I'd never be able to live with myself if I didn't try to help. Besides, that man in there's the only one who can clear my name. So I've got to find him—before it's too late."

Spud said, "Then I guess all three of us will get our first experience as spelunker's together." He looked at Ruby and smiled. "That's someone who explores caves."

"I figgered," she replied, smiling back.

Hildy squared her shoulders, resolutely facing whatever dangers she was about to encounter.

Some time later the mossy edge of the cave had been left behind. Odell led single file down rough marble stairs toward their objective four hundred feet under the earth. Ruby followed their guide. Next came Hildy, with Spud bringing up the rear.

Hildy's heart thudded so loudly she imagined she could hear it even above the hissing of the blue flame from the carbide lamp that was affixed to the miner's caps Odell had provided all four spelunkers. The light moved wherever Hildy looked. The lamp cast huge black shadows that leaped like living things. Sometimes there were double or multiple shadows as Ruby's, Spud's and Odell's lights crossed in the cave.

Hildy's lips moved in silent prayer as the terrifying sensation of claustrophobia engulfed her. She felt as though the cave was closing in on her, crushing her, smothering her. She wanted to run wildly in panic, to do anything except take one more step in the cave. But she fought against the unreasonable fear.

What was it Brother Ben had said when they left him? Something to do with fear. "Displacement's the secret, Hildy. Replace your fear thoughts with something else."

Hildy tried to force herself to think of other things besides the cool, confining cave into which she was venturing deeper and deeper. Her mind flitted from one thing to another. *Mischief's safe with Jacob and Brother Ben . . . This is the last time I'll have with Spud, maybe forever, because he's leaving tomorrow for his parents' home in New York . . . Ruby seems different since her fleece was confirmed this morning . . . That church sure won't be the same after Uncle Nate's sermon . . . I wonder if we can find this man down here before the river rises? Sure hope it doesn't come up too fast and cut us off before we can get back out!* . . . "Be not afraid, for I am with you always."

Spud said cheerfully, "Did you know that Mark Twain used one of these Mother Lode caves as the model for the one he wrote about when Tom Sawyer got lost in Missouri cave?"

Ordinarily, that would have interested Hildy. But unexplainable fear clung to her as she carefully groped her way down narrow trails, shivering in the fifty-five degree coolness.

Spud continued. "And John Muir, the famous naturalist, also explored these foothill caves. Maybe this very one. He used candles, because they didn't have flashlights or carbide lamps back then."

Hildy shuddered, thinking how easily a candle could go out. She wondered, *Can these carbide lamps run out of fuel before we get back?* She shook off the thought.

They moved on, deeper and deeper, their lights temporarily beating back the total blackness of the cave. There was no sound except an occasional dripping and the passing of the four people.

The spelunkers left the narrow marble passage behind. They stood in a small underground chamber. Hildy wondered if it would collapse and trap them. She asked, "Odell, how long's this cave been here?"

"Some authorities say close to millions of years. It was made by volcanic activity. This produced a powerful sulfuric acid solution. It was so strong it slowly ate away the underground limestone."

Odell turned his head to the right and up so his light shone high above them. "Those whitish things hanging from the walls are called flowstones."

Spud said, "They sort of look like jellyfish, from the top dome to all those parts hanging down like a mantle. Except these aren't clear like a jellyfish."

Odell kept walking. "Human bones have been found here dating back nearly thirteen thousand years. Supposed to be among the oldest remains found on this continent."

Ruby was superstitious about the dead, so she changed the subject. "Spud, is they a diff'runce atwixt a cave an' a cavern?"

He seemed pleased that she had asked. "Well, a cave's more like a hollow in the earth. It usually goes more or less horizontally into a mountain. A cavern, like this one, is a large underground cave with rooms and passages of various sizes. Some go back into the earth for miles."

Odell said, "Past the rivers and the place we're going, there's a chamber tall enough to put a ten-story building in. We won't have time to see it."

Hildy's light showed formations hanging from the chamber's roof. They looked like icicles dripping from the eaves back east. There were also formations on the floor, like inverted ice cream cones.

Spud explained, "Those hanging down are stalactites. The ones on the floor are stalagmites. They're both made over countless centuries by the dripping of water percolating through the rocks from above."

Odell stopped and produced a small stick from his backpack of ropes and spare fuel for the lights. "A cave's a very fragile thing," he explained. "You should leave a cave as you find it, and be very careful of everything. Don't try this, but listen."

He tapped a long, thin stalactite. It gave off a tiny, musical tone, like something in a fairy story. He repeated the action. When the second beautiful sound faded away, he replaced the stick and walked on.

Hildy tried to think how fascinating all this was, but her thoughts jumped again. *Whoever's down here could hear us coming or see our lights, but we wouldn't know he's there if he hid.*

If he had a carbide lamp, he could extinguish it, then relight it when we are gone. Or he could use a five-celled flashlight. Either way, she thought, *we could walk within a couple feet of him and maybe not know.* "Stop scaring yourself!" she whispered under her breath.

She estimated they had been traveling about fifteen minutes when Odell called, "Got to crawl on your knees the last few feet before we cross the first underground river . . ."

"First?" Hildy interrupted fearfully. She had not realized Odell had earlier used the plural, rivers.

"That's right," Odell replied. "There're two. When we cross the second one, we'll be near the President Washington Room. That's where X marks the spot we want."

Hildy's claustrophobia seeped over her as she thought of two underground rivers that were going to rise and flood the caverns that very afternoon. *Mustn't think about that!* she told herself.

The floor was damp and cool to her touch as she eased forward on hands and knees. The ceiling dipped to within a foot of her head. From it, many brownish-white stalactites hung down on either side of her as she crawled. There was one small white stalagmite.

Odell's light rose as he stood up again. "Here's the first river crossing. Water's barely running, so it's shallow enough to wade. Farther ahead, beyond the second river crossing and the President's Room, there's a lake a couple of acres wide. It's so clear you can see the bottom thirty, forty feet down."

Hildy breathed a prayer of thanks for being out of the low passage. She scrambled to her feet to join the others at the river's edge. She was relieved when her light showed it was more like a creek than a river.

"It's very shallow and only about twenty feet wide here,"

Odell explained. "Next crossing's half that distance."

His light tilted upward, showing a low domed ceiling of solid rock. "As you can see," the guide continued, "the ceiling's only about fifteen feet up, so in the winter, this chamber fills to the top. I don't expect it to get that high today, but this river'll be too wide, deep, and swift to cross if we delay very long in getting back."

Hildy gulped as her mind screamed, *Get out! Go back! If you keep going, you can get caught and drown when the water rises. We could all drown!* But somehow, she kept her mouth shut as Odell's light again dropped to the river.

"You can see it's already starting to rise because of the water backing up at the new dam," Odell said. "That affects both these underground rivers here."

It took all of Hildy's willpower to fight off the almost over-powering urge to run, screaming in terror, back toward the surface. Instead, with another silent prayer, she waded across the water with Odell, Ruby, and Spud.

The water barely covered their ankles. Their shoes sloshed as they stepped out and kept going.

Hildy tried to replace her fear by appreciating the natural wonders of creation few people would ever see. Her light guided her around immense stone columns, silent and majestic. She glimpsed crystal flowers of incredible and delicate beauty. It was breathtaking in every sense of the word, yet Hildy was breathing hard. She knew that was more from claustrophobia than walking.

She was pleasantly surprised when they crossed the second stream a few minutes later. Here, the water came to Hildy's calves. Its flow was swifter and more noticeable against her bare skin than the first crossing.

Hildy managed to keep her voice from quavering as she asked, "Odell, how long before it's not safe to get back?"

"Couple hours, I hope, but can't be sure. Let's hurry to the President's Room. Try to warn that guy."

Hildy didn't need any urging.

As they approached their destination, a different feeling began to creep over the girl, a sense of impending danger, different from her other fear. Squeezing through another tunnel on hands and knees, with lights showing chambers on both sides, Hildy stopped and sniffed. Her sense of danger was overpowering.

"What's the matter?" Spud asked from behind her.

Hildy sniffed again. She had gotten used to the dank smell, so she was surprised when something familiar drifted to her nostrils.

"Smells funny," she said. "I've smelled it before, but I can't place it."

Ruby sniffed, too, and said, "Not the kinda smell I'd 'spect down here."

Odell called out from ahead, "We're almost there, folks!"

Hildy scrambled forward, her uneasiness growing. She glanced around anxiously, seeing shadows jump away. If one was that of their mysterious crook, it couldn't be distinguished from the other leaping shadows.

"Just around this next corner," Odell announced, "you'll see some sights like you've never seen before."

They pressed against another glistening wall, their feet stepping over small stalagmites. They stopped side by side in a room of incredible splendor. The chamber was about fifty feet high, Hildy guessed. Stalactites hung from the ceiling like gigantic crystal decorations. But the dominant feature was an immense stalagmite.

Odell moved his head about so his light focused on the stalagmite. "Here's President Washington, in stone."

"It's magnificent!" Spud breathed. "Incredible!"

"Glorious!" Hildy agreed.

"Shore is!" Ruby whispered in an awed voice.

Odell moved his light. "This stalagmite is thirty-nine feet tall, the results of drippings started countless centuries ago. Those made Washington's features. See them? Wig, eyes, nose, mouth?"

Hildy admitted, "It does look like the drawing on the back of that picture!"

The icicle-like formations from the ceiling were mixed with

rounded stalactites of pastel pinks and pristine white. As the four lights moved by the turning of each viewer's head, other marvelous sights were revealed from what had been total darkness.

Off to the sides, away from the silent statuary, there were alcoves naturally furnished with tables, stools, and shelves. The hissing blue flames of the carbide lamps illuminated crystalline chandeliers overhead. They glittered like diamonds, creating countless points of light.

Hildy turned her head, and she gasped with delight at the strange and beautiful colors—pale blue, soft lavender and delicate pink, then fiery red and brilliant purple. But when her light moved on, the colors vanished. They were replaced by total, silent blackness.

As they moved on, Hildy became enchanted with the spectacular scenes. Her fear was less intense now as she replaced it with the marvels revealed before her eyes.

Odell turned his head so the light on his cap explored the bottom of the great piece of natural statuary. "But where's the X that marks the spot your sheriff's deputy described to our sheriff? I've poked around there without any success."

All three youngsters pointed their lights at the base. Beneath the immense domed stalagmite, countless stalactites had formed. They formed a skirt of irregular length icicles around the bottom.

Ruby said, "Could be anywhere behind those."

"Unless," Hildy added, "he's already been here, found the spot marked X on the map, and left."

Odell shrugged. Ruby's light behind him made the motion look like a giant on the glistening white wall. "Well, let's try hollering. Warn him."

"What if he can't hear us?" Hildy asked.

"This place is so quiet that voices will carry everywhere," Odell replied. "He'll hear, but whether or not he believes us and saves himself—well, here goes."

He cupped his hands, took a deep breath, and yelled, "Anybody in this cave—listen to me! The back entrance caved in. You can't get out the way you came in."

The words echoed off into the distance, slowly fading into silence. Odell yelled again, "The underground rivers will rise this afternoon. The engineers at the dam are causing the water to flow like it does in winter. This cave's filled with water by then. You've got to come out—now—or you'll drown!"

Again, the words echoed and died. Odell took another deep breath and called through cupped hands, "Come out with us now! It's your only chance!"

When only a terrible brooding silence prevailed again, Hildy shuddered. "Why doesn't he answer?"

"Maybe Hildy's right," Ruby said. "He's done gone."

"One way to find out," Odell decided. "Let's see if we can find what that X on the map means."

They spread out around the giant, silent natural wonder. Spud and Odell went to the left; Hildy and Ruby to the right. Their lights marked their positions about the base. It was bigger around than a double garage. The four hissing blue flames in reflectors probed behind and under the immense stalagmite's skirt of stone icicles.

Hildy was increasingly uneasy. She had managed to control her claustrophobic fear somewhat, but the sense of danger grew stronger. She knelt to shine her light on a five-foot-tall stalagmite that had crossed with another shorter one.

She caught her breath, wondering, *Could that be an X ?* She bent closer, looking behind the crossed stalagmites. *Nothing there*, she thought in disappointment. *Wait? What're those?*

She picked them and examined them. "I've found something!" she called. "A couple pieces of rusted metal. Looks as if they were knocked off by somebody pounding on them. Maybe from an old chest."

She heard Spud and Odell on the far side of the stalagmite as they started toward her. Ruby was instantly beside Hildy. Their combined lights focused on the metal.

Ruby exclaimed, "Reckon yore right!" Her light moved to the cave floor. She pointed. "See them scratch marks on the floor? Looks like somethin' heavy was drug thar."

Spud's light showed he was hurrying around from the other side of the huge stalagmite. He called, "Could it be from an iron strongbox stagecoaches carried?"

"I don't know," Hildy replied. She stopped and sniffed, suddenly tense. "Ruby, I smell that odor again!"

Ruby sniffed and nodded. "Yore right! But what—?"

"Now I know!" Hildy interrupted. She spun around, her light flashing about. "Remember when we went to see Alice Quayle the first time, and her boyfriend opened the door? He was all dressed up, but he smelled funny."

"Yeah!" Ruby exclaimed. "Now I remember! But what—?"

Hildy rushed on. "The kitchen ceiling had been freshly painted. Later, I saw a paint-spotted ladder outside the house. That first time, they were getting ready to leave for San Francisco, and Bob'd cleaned up. But he had to use turpentine to clean his paint brushes, and he couldn't get the turpentine smell off his hands. That's what I smelled when he grabbed me outside the brush arbor."

Ruby nodded. "Yeah! That's when ye bit his finger, but Alice later said he claimed he'd hurt his finger crankin' an ol' car!"

Hildy glanced around nervously. "That's what we smell now. Turpentine. That means he's here, Ruby!"

A man's voice said from behind a large stalagmite, "You're right. I'm here, and I've got what I came for. But I need help getting it out."

Bob Medwin turned a powerful flashlight's beam on the girls, partially blinding them, but not before Hildy saw the scrawny young man in carpenter's white duck overalls and heavy work shoes.

He raised his voice. "Everybody stop right where you are and stand still so nobody gets hurt!"

Hildy heard Spud and Odell stop. In the light of the girls' carbide lamps, Hildy saw that Bob Medwin wore the same frayed blue denim shirt and plaid golf cap he'd had on when he knocked her down on the sidewalk that day.

Medwin tilted the many-celled flashlight up, the powerful beam blinding the girls. "All right," he growled. "You two, get over here and give me a hand with this!"

He raised his voice. "You two guys over there, stay back! You hear me?"

"We hear you," Odell answered.

"Good!" Medwin lowered his voice. His flashlight flickered down at his feet, showing a very old chest about two feet long and a foot high. "You girls grab the front end."

As Hildy bent to obey, she caught a whiff of turpentine from his clothes. "Where we going?" she asked.

"Out of here before the rivers cut us off."

"What about them?" She jerked her head toward Spud and Odell. Their lights weren't moving.

"They can follow from a distance. Nobody needs to get hurt if everyone does what I say. Now move, or none of us'll get out of here alive! I can hear the river rising!"

Hildy heard it, too, and her heart nearly stopped.

CHAPTER
TWENTY-ONE

UP FROM THE DEPTHS
OF THE EARTH

As the girls staggered toward the first river, the rusted iron handle of the heavy chest cut into their fingers. The cousins could each get only two fingers on the rough handle. They walked ahead of their captor, who carried the back end of the box with his left hand. His right held a powerful five-celled flashlight.

As they approached the first underground river, Hildy's mouth dried with fear. She hadn't even noticed any sound from the river when they had crossed earlier. Now its rushing sound was ominous. As they neared the stream, Hildy's and Ruby's carbide lights revealed a dramatic change between the shallow, placid underground river of a little while before and the surging water now blocking their way to safety.

"Don't just stand there! Get across!" Medwin snapped behind them.

Cautiously, Hildy obeyed, easing her feet into the stream. Ruby did the same. The rising water was so swift it threatened to sweep both girls off balance.

"Don't be scared!" Hildy whispered as each step brought the water higher on her legs.

"Who's skeered?" Ruby asked, but she didn't sound convincing.

"Shut up, you two!" Medwin ordered from where he held the other end of the box. "We're wasting time!"

Panting with their efforts, the girls finally were across the stream and onto the cave floor again.

"We'uns done made it!" Ruby exclaimed.

"So far, so good," Hildy answered. Her two fingers hurt from the weight of the iron box and its contents. She said, "We need to stop and rest our fingers!"

"Shore do! My fingers is plumb wore out!" Ruby added.

"No stopping!" the man commanded. "You saw that river. The second one's going to be worse. Move!"

Hildy said a silent prayer as she lurched forward. She stole a glance back. The twin carbide lamps marked Spud's and Odell's positions. They were well back, but still coming.

Hildy muttered, "If there was just some way we could get away from this guy!"

"Shut up!" Medwin snapped. "Save your breath!"

Hildy couldn't help thinking about the river ahead. *It's twice as wide, maybe now twice as deep! Even if we make it with this box, what about Spud and Odell?*

Each step became a nightmare of thought. *Is this the right way back? I don't remember that column. Odell led us in, but he's been here many times before. Medwin's got the map, but it's not very clear.*

Hildy's train of thought came to a halt as Ruby whispered, "What'd ye reckon's in this ol' box? Gold?"

"Gold's so heavy I don't think we could carry it."

"Well, then, why'd them stagecoach fellers need sech a heavy box?"

"I don't know. Spud said it's called a strongbox, but I don't know what's in it."

"Shut up, I said!" Medwin hissed.

The girls fell silent. They were suffering from the forced march and weight of the box on their aching fingers. When again they had to get down on hands and knees to squeeze through a low overhead tunnel, Hildy and Ruby changed hands on the box while working some circulation back into their aching fingers. Then they stood and hurried again, not so much afraid of their captor's warnings as what the next river crossing might mean.

Bob Medwin hurried them at a fast, almost reckless pace. He did not speak, but Hildy could hear his hard breathing.

She also heard something else. She cocked her head to listen, sending her light off sharply to the side. She lowered her voice. "I have an idea!"

"What?"

"When we get into the middle of the next river, you let go the box when I say so!"

"Drop it?" Ruby whispered in disbelief.

"It's our only chance! Because when he gets this box to where he can handle it by himself, he won't need us anymore. Besides, we could identify him."

"But he done said nobody's goin' to git hurt."

"We can't trust him! So wait for my signal."

Hildy focused on the idea that had formed in the back of her mind. She reviewed it quickly, searching for any flaws. There were some bad ones. "If I'm wrong," she muttered, "it could be all over for all of us!"

She shook her head, scolding herself again. *Don't think about that! Think of something else.*

It was an effort, but images flashed through her mind. *"Spud leaving . . . Is Ruby changed? What'll happen now that her fleece test has been met? Will she and Uncle Nate go to the Ozarks? Can I go with them? I'd sure like to make up with Granny . . . What'll I get Molly for her birthday? Time's about run out.*

The sound of the river ahead washed all other thoughts away from Hildy's mind. *It's up, way up!* she thought. *Oh, Lord, help us all to get across safely!*

The placid river of an hour or so before was now building to a dull but growing roar. The moment the cousins' feet touched it, the swift current made both girls stagger.

"Keep going!" Medwin yelled.

Hildy gulped with fear as each step took her deeper into the river. *Over my ankles,* she thought. *My calves . . . knees . . . and still rising!*

A moment later Ruby whispered, "I'm skeered! It's plumb up to muh waist!"

Hildy had a hard time hearing her cousin. That made Hildy realize Medwin wouldn't be able to hear her voice above the river's increasing rumble.

Hildy didn't whisper, but did lower her voice. "I think we're more than halfway there. Yes. Feel it? The water's dropping slightly."

"Yeah, it's a-goin' down a mite."

"You ready to drop the box?"

"I'm ready. Then what?"

"Do what I do." She took a deep breath. "Now!"

Both girls let go of the rusted metal handle. The front end dropped hard into the water. The unexpected action threw Medwin off balance.

"Hey!" he cried, staggering forward under the full weight of the box. Then the swift current caught it and swept it sideways. Medwin was forced to drop his flashlight and use both hands to hang on to the box.

Hildy didn't see anymore. She turned and waded as fast as possible toward the far shore with Ruby beside her. Hildy didn't dare look back for fear she'd lose her balance. It was only when she crawled out on the far shore, panting hard from exertion and fear, that she glanced back to the middle of the river.

Her carbide lamp showed the heavy box was being swept downstream by the strengthening tide. The box had pulled Medwin down to where his face was just inches above the water's rough surface.

"Let go!" Hildy cried through cupped hands. "Let go of the box and save yourself!"

"No! I—" Water entering his open mouth cut his words off.

Ruby shrieked, "He's a-gonna drown hisself!"

The girls' lights showed the man's back was arched and his shoulder muscles moving in desperate efforts to hang on to the heavy box. He staggered and fell face first into the water. His whole body disappeared.

Hildy started wading back into the stream.

Ruby cried, "What air ye a-doin'?"

"Trying to help him!"

The surging power of the stream caught her feet and knocked her down. She fell backward, arms flailing. Just before she went under, dousing the blue flame of her lamp, she saw Medwin's body surge violently upward. He gasped for breath. His hands were empty.

Hildy surfaced, gasping for air. The cap and lamp had been knocked off her head. Only Ruby's carbide light on shore shone in the cave's blackness. The lamp made grotesque shadows on the low ceiling as Hildy was swept downstream by the river's fury.

She didn't know how to swim, but her need to survive made her dog-paddle and kick hard. She felt bottom and dragged herself, gasping and spitting water, onto the cave floor. She saw a carbide lamp above her. She was grabbed by both arms and pulled to safety.

"That war a plumb dumb thing to do!" Ruby growled.

Hildy couldn't argue with that. But she didn't have the breath to do so anyway. She looked around. Two lights showed that Spud and Odell were across the river. As they stood up, looking toward the girls, their lights showed something else.

"Medwin!" Hildy exclaimed, sitting up and staring downstream. He lay face down on the cave floor, legs in the water. Hildy asked fearfully, "Is he—?"

Her sentence broke off as he moved. He tried to pull himself to a sitting position, but couldn't.

"Yeah," Ruby said with grim satisfaction, "he's alive an' goin' to jail! But without his ol' box!"

Hildy looked up and laughed with relief as Spud and Odell ran up. Spud knelt to look anxiously into Hildy's face with his carbide lamp. Odell ran on toward Medwin.

"You okay, Hildy?" Spud asked anxiously.

She nodded, glancing over to see Odell take out a piece of rope from his backpack.

He raised his voice. "I'll have this feller hog-tied in two seconds, folks! Then we're getting out of here while the getting's good!"

———

Two days later, Hildy sat beside the Rickenbacker on the main highway just outside of Lone River, with Mischief perched on her neck as usual. Elizabeth and Martha thanked a customer who'd stopped to buy a watermelon.

Elizabeth handed Hildy a dime. "That's the last melon. How much money do we have altogether?"

Hildy opened the drawstring on her Bull Durham sack, dropped the coin in, and pulled the string. She laid the sack beside three others.

"After Daddy gets his share and gives you girls some money, I'll have enough to pay my tithe and buy Molly a nice birthday present."

As the sisters rose to take apart the boards and boxes they'd used for benches and put them and their signs in the Rickenbacker, Hildy's mind jumped back. "Wish Mr. Taggett'd say he was sorry for calling me an Okie, but I guess some people never change. Still, everything else turned out nice."

Spud was on his way to his parents' place again after a tender goodbye and a promise to write to Hildy.

Ruby and her father were growing closer every day and talking about going to the Ozarks for a visit.

When a deputy had arrived to arrest Bob Medwin, he confessed everything. He was a used-car salesman who wanted to marry Alice Quayle. The Depression made car selling slow, so he'd been painting Alice's house in his spare time.

On the Saturday afternoon she received the watch, he'd persuaded Alice to pawn it to get money for a trip to San Francisco. On Monday morning, the law clerk, Merle Lamar, came to the office early before his employer arrived. Lamar found Effie Baines' codicil, which he had failed to properly file with her will. Lamar phoned Medwin at Alice's home and relayed the news about the possible treasure map hidden in the watch. Later, the attorney fired Merle Lamar for dishonesty.

With no time to plan, Medwin greedily thought only of recovering the watch and the map before Taggett sold it. Alice,
who was downtown that morning, had no idea of her boyfriend's part in the watch theft.

Medwin had no money to redeem the watch, so he decided
to steal it. He quickly cleaned the paint from his hands with
turpentine, rushed in to Taggett's pawnshop, and grabbed the
watch. "The rest," he said to Hildy and friends, "you already
know."

Hildy sighed, thinking how she had suspected Dick Archer,
a painter she'd never even seen. "But," Hildy told herself, "it's
all over." She glanced up as a car slowed. *Well, maybe it's not all
over!* Hildy thought as she recognized the woman driver.

"It's Alice Quayle!" Hildy exclaimed. "She's going to be mad
because I helped send her boyfriend to jail." Hildy turned and
whispered to Elizabeth and Martha, "Go find Daddy!"

Her father had gone down the road to talk to a rancher who
was mending fence.

As the two sisters ran off, Hildy gulped and stood up to face
her visitor.

Alice glanced at the coon riding on Hildy's shoulders before
lowering her eyes to meet Hildy's. The woman said, "I've got
something for you." She reached into her purse.

Hildy tensed, but before she could say anything, Alice's hand
reappeared from her purse. She held out a lady's gold watch
and chain.

"Here," she said, pushing it into Hildy's hand. "I want you
to have it. It's the least I can do after all this watch put you
through. And it's also to thank you for helping me find out what
kind of man Bob was before I made the mistake of marrying
him."

Hildy's mouth dropped open as the woman turned, leaving
the watch in the girl's hands.

Later, as her father drove the girls toward the barn-house,
Hildy examined the watch while her mind soared. *Some people
say it was all Spud's hard work putting out flyers with the Benton kids*

that helped fill the church for Uncle Nate. But I know better. Sure, that helped, and so did prayer and other things, but the Lord packed that church.

Hildy's father asked from the front seat, "What're you thinking about?"

"Huh? Oh, lots of things. Like what happened after the underground rivers dropped in the cave and Odell Shanley found the box Bob Medwin had forced Ruby and me to help him carry."

Her father chuckled. "I'd like to have seen Medwin's face when he was told what the secret of Howling Cave really was! Just an old strongbox filled with Confederate currency. It's not even worth one penny."

Hildy smiled. "I was also thinking how Mr. Farnham drove out to our place and apologized for misjudging me. And about him choosing me to be his part-time hired girl after school starts."

Elizabeth said, "Then you can start saving for college, and our forever home. But mostly, I'll bet you're glad your name's cleared."

Hildy agreed. "What's the Scripture say about that? 'A good name is rather to be chosen than great riches.' "

Her father nodded. "Yes, but sometimes a person has to fight to keep that good name. Hildy, I'm proud of how you did that."

"Yes," Elizabeth agreed, "because our name's Corrigan too."

"Thanks!" Hildy gave her sister a quick hug. Then Hildy leaned back, petting her coon with one hand and holding the watch in the other. "Now I can give Molly the really special birthday present I wanted for her—and have money left over."

Hildy felt good. All but a couple of prayers she'd written down had been answered. She expected those would be answered too, maybe before school started. September was almost here. The Corrigans hadn't even been in California three full months, yet so many exciting things had happened in spite of the Depression. Surely lots more was ahead.

Yes, Hildy thought, *I'm sure of it!*

She leaned back in the backseat as the Rickenbacker continued on toward the Corrigan home.

ACKNOWLEDGEMENTS

This novel would not be possible without the cooperation of various people to whom the author extends his heartfelt thanks. Among these are:

- Barbara Munson, Secretary-Treasurer of the National Caves Association, McMinnville, Tennessee;
- Steve fairchild, owner of three caves: the Boyden Caverns, California Caverns, and Moaning Cavern.

While those named above were helpful in providing some authentic background material for this book, the author is solely responsible for the accuracy of details in this work. However, the author did take limited literary license in the interest of adding drama to the story.